The Feelings We Can't Hide

A Novel

by Veronika Dean

The Feelings We Can't Hide

This is a work of fiction. Names, characters, places, and incidents are products of the author's imagination or are used fictitiously. Any resemblance to actual persons, living or dead, or actual events is purely coincidental.

Cover design by Veronika Dean

ISBN: 978-1-972938-00-3

Published by Veronika Dean

Table of Contents

For the ones who found their voice after the silence.
And for anyone who ever chose themselves.

Chapter 1

Maya's POV

Maya tucked a strand of hair behind her ear as she followed her roommate, Shelby, down the store aisle. Shelby was in full grocery-shopping mode, scanning the shelves like a woman on a mission.

"Pasta, check. Spinach, check..." Shelby muttered to herself, checking the items in the cart. Maya, on the other hand, was mentally checking out. Her mind drifted as they passed the snack aisle, her eyes catching on a familiar blue bag.

"I'll be right back," Maya said, already heading in that direction. Shelby didn't even look up as she waved her off.

Without the cart, Maya slipped easily through the other customers, making a beeline for her guilty pleasure—kettle-cooked chips. Grabbing a bag, she smiled to herself and turned back toward the main aisle.

She barely took three steps before rounding the corner too fast.

And that's when she collided with something solid—some*one* solid.

A strong arm shot out, grabbing her waist as she stumbled back, her chips flying out of her hands. The sudden jolt left her breathless, and it took her a second to realize whose arm was now steadying her.

Ryan. Ryan Taylor.

She froze. His grip on her waist was firm, keeping her from falling completely, and his touch was unexpectedly warm. Her eyes snapped up to meet his, those hazel eyes filled with surprise and concern.

"Maya?" Ryan's voice was low, familiar. He let her go as soon as she regained her balance.

"Ryan," she managed, her voice smaller than she would've liked. Her heart thudded in her chest, not entirely from the near fall.

A small box of cereal lay at his feet—the casualty of their collision. Much less dramatic than the situation itself.

Before Maya could say anything more, a voice she knew too well pierced the tension.

"Maya?" Cole spoke, echoing through her mind.

A cold wave rushed through her before she even turned around. She should have known that Ryan's presence here meant Cole's as well.

Cole stood a few feet away, the same sharp jawline, the same deep-set eyes that once felt like home.

And for a split second—before the awkward tension, before the weight of everything that went wrong settled in her chest—she was somewhere else entirely.

A year ago, the store had been nearly empty, just the two of them wandering the aisles, hands intertwined, laughing over some dumb debate about ice cream flavors.

"I'm just saying," Cole had argued, waving a pint of chocolate chip cookie dough in the air, "you can't call it 'cookie dough' if the dough bits are tiny."

Maya snorted, nudging his side. "That's literally the whole point. It's supposed to be bite-sized."

Cole scoffed. "No, see, if I want cookie dough, I want actual chunks to be in there. Not these little—" He shook the pint again for emphasis. "—specks."

Maya rolled her eyes, grabbing a tub of her usual. "Fine. More for me, then."

Cole's mock offense lasted all of five seconds before he leaned in, pressing a kiss to her temple, his voice dropping to that low, teasing tone that always sent warmth curling through her. "You're lucky you're cute, you know."

Maya had laughed, looping her arms around his waist in the middle of the frozen food section. It had been so easy back then—light, simple, effortless.

She remembered thinking, 'This is it. This is what love is supposed to feel like.'

NOW, STANDING IN THE same store, staring at the same man who had once kissed her like she was his whole world, Maya felt an ache she hadn't been prepared for.

Because it hadn't all been bad.

Because once upon a time, Cole had been someone she trusted—someone she *loved.*

And now?

Now, she could barely hold his gaze without remembering why they'd fallen apart.

Her heart sank. She turned, already knowing what she'd see.

Cole stood a few feet away, looking between her and Ryan with an expression that mirrored Ryan's surprise but carried an extra weight of history.

Ryan bent down to pick up the fallen cereal, but Maya didn't miss the way his hand brushed against hers when he straightened up.

Great. Of all the grocery stores, of all the aisles, it had to be this one.

Maya swallowed hard, the air around her thick with awkward tension.

"Hey, Cole," she said, forcing a tight smile. She tucked her hair behind her ear, a nervous habit she hadn't shaken.

Cole crossed his arms, his eyes shifting from Maya to Ryan. "Didn't expect to see you here," he said, his voice neutral but with a tinge of something she couldn't place.

"Yeah, small world," Maya replied, not quite steady. She looked at Ryan, who was now standing awkwardly, holding the box of cereal as though it were a shield. "Sorry about that," she said, gesturing to the box.

Ryan shook his head, the corner of his mouth lifting into a faint smile. "Don't worry about it. Happens." His voice was calm, but Maya didn't miss the way his eyes lingered on her, almost like he was trying to figure out how to handle the situation.

Cole cleared his throat, breaking the moment. "Well... Ryan and I were just grabbing a few things before game night." He shifted his weight, clearly trying to regain control of the conversation.

"Oh," Maya replied, her stomach sinking. Game night. She used to be part of that—back when things were simpler, back when Cole and she were still... them.

"You, uh... here with Shelby?" Ryan asked, cutting through the awkward silence. He seemed genuinely interested, even if his tone was casual.

Maya nodded. "Yeah, she's over there somewhere, stocking up on kale or something equally healthy," she said, trying to lighten the mood.

Ryan smiled—a real smile this time—and it made her face feel warm. "That sounds about right."

Cole shifted again, his eyes narrowing slightly at Ryan before turning back to Maya. "Well, we should—"

"Right," Maya interrupted, not wanting to drag this out any longer. "I should get back to Shelby. But... good to see you both."

Ryan's eyes met hers again, and for a split second, something unspoken passed between them, but it was gone as quickly as it came.

"Yeah, you too," Ryan said softly.

Cole gave her a quick nod, and before Maya said anything more, she turned and hurried back down the aisle, her pulse racing as if she'd just escaped a close call.

Maya and Shelby finished their shopping relatively quickly, never discussing this encounter. Maya spent that time trying to focus and slow her heart rate.

She hadn't even realized she'd left her chips behind.

Ryan's POV

Ryan shoved his hands into his jacket pockets as they walked out of the store, the crisp air biting at his face. He barely noticed the cold, though. His mind was stuck on what had just happened in the snack aisle.

Maya. Of all people to run into today, it had to be her.

"You good?" Cole cut through his thoughts.

Ryan blinked, looking over at his best friend. Cole was tossing the grocery bags into the back of his car, his movements tense. "Yeah, I'm fine," Ryan muttered, more concerned about how Cole was reacting to the sudden encounter with his ex after months of no contact whatsoever.

Cole slammed the trunk closed, glancing at him with a frown. "You didn't say much back there. Kinda weird, huh?"

Ryan shrugged. "Definitely wasn't expecting to see her, that's for sure." That wasn't a lie. Seeing Maya had been like getting hit with a punch he didn't see coming. She looked... different. Happier? No, not exactly. Ryan wanted her to be happy but knew that the awkwardness between Cole and Maya was likely far from over.

He and Maya had been good friends when she was still dating Cole, but their relationship had naturally drifted off with their breakup. After all, Ryan was likely a reminder to Maya of Cole and, of course, Ryan was expected to be on Cole's "side" though that time as well.

"Yeah," Cole said, his tone flat. "It's whatever." He opened the driver's side door and slid in without another word, leaving Ryan standing there for a moment, staring at the car as if it could tell him if Cole was going to start obsessing over Maya again like he did following their split.

Ryan exhaled, running a hand through his hair before he finally climbed in the passenger seat. Cole started the engine, and they pulled out of the parking lot in silence. The only sound was the low hum of the radio and the occasional rustle of the bags in the back.

His thoughts drifted again—to the way Maya had stumbled into him, the way her wide eyes had flashed with surprise before she'd gone stiff in his arms. It had been a split second, but he could still feel the softness of her waist under his hand, see the guardedness in her expression, and he hated that she felt she needed to be on guard.

Cole cleared his throat, bringing him back to reality. "So, I think we're ready for game night, right?"

"Yeah," Ryan replied. After all, game nights were typically automatic. Pizza, beer, and a few rounds of video games with the guys. But tonight? He was still waiting to see a real reaction out of Cole.

"Cool," Cole said, casual but still carrying that edge Ryan couldn't quite ignore. "I think some of the guys might be bringing their girlfriends. Could be a full house."

Ryan nodded, staring out the window, not really caring about who would be there. His thoughts were still tangled in what had happened back in the store. He hadn't seen Maya much since she and Cole broke up. She'd pretty much vanished from their circle. It was weird at first—her absence. Like a limb was missing that no one wanted to talk about.

And now she was back. At least, for that moment.

He glanced at Cole out of the corner of his eye. Cole hadn't seemed too bothered by it all, but Ryan knew better. Cole wasn't the type to let on when something was really getting to him. And for all his cool indifference, Ryan could tell Maya showing up had gotten under his skin.

They pulled up to the house, and Ryan grabbed the grocery bags from the backseat, following Cole up the front steps. The house was already buzzing with the familiar sound of laughter and music filtering out through the cracked windows.

The door swung open, and Cole led the way inside, immediately getting pulled into a conversation with one of their friends.

Ryan sighed, heading to the kitchen to dump everything and ignore the nagging feelings in the back of his mind.

Maya's POV

Groceries put away, Maya returned to her room. The afternoon light slanted through the window as she sat down at her desk, her portfolio spread out in front of her. She'd been working on it for months, refining each piece, but today her mind wasn't on the work. Her thoughts kept drifting back to Cole—their talks about settling down, starting a family, and the life he'd envisioned for them. It was everything she had once thought she wanted.

But then, the walls started to close in.

They had sat in their old apartment months ago, her chest tightening as she tried to find the words. "Cole, I've been thinking... about my career. I am going to apply to a few positions in New York."

Cole had barely looked up from his laptop. "I thought we talked about this, Maya. We agreed we'd stay here, close to my family. We're supposed to be building a life together."

Maya had felt the weight of his expectations pressing down on her. "But that's not what I agreed to, Cole, and you know it."

Cole had looked up then, his face hardening. "You said you wanted kids. A family. What do you mean you didn't agree?"

Her throat had tightened, the words almost too heavy to say. "That hasn't changed. I just... I want my own life, too, before all that. I don't want to lose myself."

"We can't just live in your parents' backyard forever," she had said, her voice barely above a whisper.

"What's wrong with my family?" Cole had replied, his eyes narrowing. "They support us. You know how much that means to me."

But to Maya, it had felt like the end. Of her making her own decisions. Of her being able to think for herself. Of him even pretending to support her dreams.

The memory stung even now, sitting at her desk with her portfolio. She had chosen her career, her independence, over Cole, but the decision still weighed on her. Even as she sent out applications to New York, part of her wondered—had she made the right choice?

She sighed, opening her laptop. She hadn't thought about the breakup for months now. She had pushed it from her mind, interested only in these last few months until graduation. It was just like Cole to show up now, out of the blue, and distract her. Maya pursed her lips for a moment, refocusing. She wasn't about to let that happen.

Chapter 2

Ryan's POV

Ryan tugged his jacket tighter around him as the crisp wind cut through the air, spring finally making an appearance. He blew into his coffee cup, enjoying the warmth against his hands as he stepped out of the cozy little coffee shop on campus. His morning so far had been a blur, and caffeine was a necessary lifeline if he had any hope of making it through his afternoon classes.

He barely noticed the figure approaching the corner at the same time as him until they almost collided. He stopped short, his brain taking a split second to process.

Maya.

Again.

She looked up from her phone, her lips parting in surprise, and Ryan almost laughed at the absurdity of it all.

"Are you following me now, or what?" he joked, a grin tugging at the corners of his mouth. He tried to keep it light, but he was genuinely surprised to see her again. What were the odds?

Maya's eyes widened for a second before she rolled them, a smile breaking through as she shifted her own reusable coffee cup to her other hand. "Oh, totally," came her reply, dripping with sarcasm. "I've made it my mission to find every place you go and awkwardly run into you."

Ryan chuckled, shaking his head. "Well, mission accomplished."

She laughed too, and for a moment, it was easy. Normal. Like they hadn't just spent the last few months as distant parts of the same world.

"What are you doing over here?" she asked, stuffing one hand into her jacket pocket as she fell into step beside him.

Ryan glanced at her, noticing the rosy tint to her cheeks from the crisp air. "Got a class over in Clarkson Hall. Thought I'd grab some coffee first."

"Clarkson?" She raised an eyebrow. "That's where I'm headed."

He shot her a sideways look. "So, you *are* following me."

Maya grinned, nudging him lightly with her elbow. "Don't flatter yourself, Taylor. I've got my own life, you know."

The banter was easy, and Ryan couldn't help but think how much he had missed this over the last several months.

"So," she continued, blowing into her coffee before taking a sip, "how's life with the guys? Game nights are still a thing, I hear?"

"Yeah," Ryan said, kicking at a stray rock in their path. "Pretty much the same. Cole's still pretty much undefeated, if you were wondering."

Maya laughed, and it was a sound Ryan hadn't realized he'd missed. "I'm not surprised. You guys should've banned him years ago."

"Trust me, we've thought about it."

There was a pause as they crossed the street, the wind picking up around them, rustling through the trees. Ryan glanced at her, watching the way her hair whipped around her face before she tucked it back under her scarf.

"So," he said, breaking the silence, "how've you been?"

Maya hesitated, her smile faltering slightly. "Good. Busy, but... good."

Ryan nodded, feeling the same shift. There was more to that answer, but he wasn't sure if he should push. "Yeah. I get that."

Another gust of wind whipped by, and Maya shivered slightly, clutching her coffee closer to her chest. "Ugh, I hate how long it's staying cold this year," she muttered.

Ryan looked over at her, a protective instinct kicking in. "Here." He pulled off his beanie before he could think too much about it, holding it out to her.

Maya blinked in surprise. "You don't have to—"

"Just take it," he said, trying to sound nonchalant. "I've got coffee. I'll survive."

She hesitated for a moment, then took it, slipping it over her wild hair. It was a bit big on her, but somehow, it looked right. She gave him a small, grateful smile as they kept walking.

As they approached the building, he stole a quick glance at her.

Before parting ways, he couldn't help but comment, "I didn't realize you had such a small head. Make sure that thing doesn't go flying off."

Maya was still laughing as they parted ways to go to their classes.

Maya's POV

Maya stepped out of Clarkson Hall, Ryan's beanie still on her head to hide her wind mussed hair. That's what she told herself. The chill in the air had subsided a little, but the scent of Ryan lingered even after her coffee had run out.

She tugged it down tighter, breathing in the faint scent of pine and something distinctly him that she had never noticed before. She tucked her hair behind her ear as she walked, her fingers brushing the soft fabric.

It didn't take long before she spotted her roommate leaning against her beat-up old car, arms crossed, and eyes locked on Maya the second she came into view.

"Okay, what's the story?" Shelby asked, skipping all forms of a greeting. She arched an eyebrow, her eyes zeroing in on to Maya's head like an accusation. "*That* is not yours."

Maya sighed, already feeling the interrogation coming. "It's Ryan's," she said, trying to sound casual as she opened the passenger door and tossed her bag inside.

"Ryan's?" Shelby responded with equal parts disbelief and curiosity. "As in Cole's best friend Ryan Taylor, *that* Ryan?"

Maya slid into the car, not looking at her as she fastened her seatbelt. "Yeah, that Ryan."

Shelby didn't move. "And why exactly do you have his beanie?" She spoke through the still open door.

Maya groaned, leaning her head back against the seat. "We ran into each other before class. It was cold, and he gave it to me. No big deal."

"Oh, honey," Shelby said, her tone dripping with amusement now. She finally climbed into the driver's seat, starting the engine with a grin. "That is *so* a big deal."

"It's not," Maya insisted, regardless of how much she had missed her friend. "We've run into each other a couple of times this week. Once at the store, and now today. That's it. He's allowed to be my friend, too."

"The store?" Shelby's head whipped around. "When did this happen?"

Maya sighed, realizing she'd accidentally opened a can of worms. "On Saturday. I was getting chips, and I bumped into Ryan. Cole was there, too."

Shelby's eyes widened. "Wait, you didn't tell me you saw Cole!"

"I didn't think it was a big deal," Maya mumbled, suddenly feeling very self-conscious. Shelby's eyes were practically burning a hole in her now. "It was awkward, we said hi, and then I left. End of story."

Shelby wasn't buying it. "Uh-huh. And now you've got Ryan's hat. I'm telling you; there's something going on here."

"There's not," Maya shot back, rolling her eyes. "I'm pretty sure he would have given it to you if you wanted."

Shelby smirked, clearly unconvinced. "Right. Sure. So, are you planning on giving it back? Or, I don't know, keeping it as a souvenir of your *totally random* run-ins with Ryan?"

Maya rolled her eyes again, fearing this conversation might get them stuck in that position. "I'll give it back."

"When?" Shelby pressed, reversing out of the parking lot. "I mean, how long are you planning to just hang onto it? If you wear it to class tomorrow, I'm calling it."

"I'm *not* wearing it tomorrow," Maya said, though part of her did wonder when she'd even see Ryan again. "I'll figure it out."

Shelby grinned, the teasing glint still in her eyes. "I'm just saying, you've got options here."

Maya didn't reply, instead staring out the window as the scenery blurred by. Options. The thought stuck with her, though she had never thought of Ryan that way.

The next day, Maya stood outside the small, quiet campus library where Ryan worked part-time, the warm, soft fabric of his hat clenched in her fists. This was no big deal. She and Ryan had had plenty of one-on-one conversations over the years. They were friends and that shouldn't have to change because of Cole.

She exhaled, pushing the door open. The warmth of the library hit her immediately, and the scent of old books filled the air. She spotted Ryan behind the circulation desk, leaning back in his chair, headphones in as he lazily scrolled through his phone. His relaxed posture, the way his shirt clung to his broad shoulders—she had to laugh at the seriousness with which he took his job.

Before she could muffle the sound, he looked up and noticed her. His face shifted from casual boredom to surprise, then to a smile while she composed herself. He pulled out one earbud as she approached.

"Maya," he said breaking the silence of the otherwise hushed space. "Hey."

She smiled back. "Hey," she said, lifting the hat slightly. "I, uh, wanted to give this back."

Ryan's eyes flicked to the fabric, a small smirk tugging at his lips. "You sure? Looks like you've gotten awfully comfortable with it."

Maya made a face, falling easily back into their typical teasing banter. "I'm not planning to steal it, if that's what you're implying."

He chuckled softly, taking it from her hands, his fingers brushing hers for just a second.

"So," he said, setting the beanie aside but not putting it away. His eyes stayed on her. "What brings you here? I mean, you could've returned it after class. Or, you know... not at all."

Maya felt her neck getting warm. "I just... figured it was easier this way."

His smirk widened. "Sure. Easier."

There was something in his tone—something playful, but also pointed, like he could see right through her. It made her heart rate increase.

"Are you here alone?" she asked, softer than she intended.

Ryan nodded, leaning on the counter now, his full attention on her. "Yeah, it's pretty dead on Wednesdays. Just me until closing."

Dead. Alone. Maya's mind flickered to the fact that there was no one around, no prying eyes, and no influence of Cole hanging over this conversation.

She shifted her feet. "Nice. Sounds... peaceful."

Ryan's gaze was intense now, his eyes searching her face like he was trying to figure something out. The playful teasing had slipped away, replaced by a silence that was heavy with unspoken words.

"It can be," he said quietly, his tone lower now. "But sometimes, it's kind of lonely."

Maya's breath caught in her throat. His words hung between them, loaded in a manner she wasn't used to with Ryan.

For a second, she felt pulled in. Pulled closer to him, like the space between them was shrinking. His presence was grounding, familiar, but also felt different than it used to.

This was dangerous. She knew it. Cole would have a conniption, she was sure, to see them now.

So much for Cole not having any influence on their conversation.

And yet, she couldn't bring herself to step back. She wondered if there was something Ryan wanted to say while also debating if it was still her place to ask.

"Ryan," she said softly, barely above a whisper. She wasn't even sure what she was trying to say.

He didn't answer. Instead, he shifted, standing up straighter and leaning slightly over the counter. The movement was subtle but enough to close some of the distance between them. For a moment, she thought he would speak.

Suddenly, she remembered that this was Cole's best friend. She needed to keep some distance between them, physically and mentally. For her own sanity.

"I should go," she said, her words quicker than she wanted.

Ryan blinked, clearly thrown off by the sudden shift. "Maya—"

"I'll see you around," she interrupted, forcing a smile that didn't reach her eyes. She turned on her heel, practically rushing toward the door before she could second-guess herself.

The cold air hit her hard as she stepped outside, but it wasn't enough to cool the warmth that had rushed to her face, her skin still tingling from the proximity to Ryan.

She didn't stop walking until she was well out of sight from the library, pressure building in her chest for reasons she couldn't quite explain.

Ryan was her friend, but he was Cole's first and foremost, and it would behoove her to not forget that.

Chapter 3

Maya's POV

By the time Maya got home, the sensation of Ryan's presence had long faded, but the weight of the moment still clung to her. The cool evening air had done little to clear her head. She shut the door behind her with a soft click, leaning back against it, eyes closed as she exhaled slowly.

"Maya?" Shelby's call echoed from the kitchen. There was the sound of water running, then the clink of dishes being set aside. "Is that you?"

Maya inhaled, pushing off the door. "Yeah, it's me."

Shelby appeared in the doorway, drying her hands on a dish towel. With one look at Maya, her brow furrowed with suspicion. "You look... weird. What happened?"

Maya sank onto the couch after kicking off her shoes. "Nothing happened."

Shelby didn't buy it. She perched herself on the arm of the chair opposite the couch, arms crossed, gaze fixed on Maya. "Liar. I know you too well. Spill it."

Maya hesitated, running her hand through her hair, her mind circling the library scene with Ryan. But there was also something else lurking in her thoughts—something older, more complicated.

"I went to return Ryan's beanie," Maya started, keeping her tone even.

Shelby's eyebrows shot up. "And?"

"And... I don't know." Maya let out a long breath. "It got weird."

Shelby's curiosity sharpened. "Weird how? Like awkward weird, or 'something's going on' weird?"

Maya chewed on her lip, staring at a spot on the carpet. "I really don't know."

Shelby's eyes widened. "Okay, I'm going to need more than that. What happened?"

Maya leaned her head back against the couch, quieter now. "We were alone. It was just the two of us in the library, and there was this moment where... I don't know, it felt like he wanted to say something but never did."

"And then you...?"

"Bailed," Maya admitted, squeezing her eyes shut. "He's Cole's best friend. As much as I wish things were different, that's reality."

Shelby groaned, sliding down onto the couch next to her. "Oh my god. Maya!"

"I panicked, okay?" Maya sighed, turning to face Shelby. "I haven't seen any of those guys in months and it's just been easier that way."

Shelby stared at her, clearly trying to read between the lines. "Easier because it's Ryan? Or because of Cole?"

Maya groaned at the mention of his name. Cole. Her ex. The boy who had been everything for so long. For four years, they had been inseparable, a picture-perfect couple, always planning, always talking about the future. Graduation, moving in together, starting their lives. It had all seemed so certain, so easy—until it wasn't.

She could still remember how he'd looked at her during their last conversation. The hurt in his eyes, the sharp edges of his words. It hadn't been one fight, one blowout. It had been a series of cracks over time, splintering what they had built together. And then... it was over.

But she couldn't bring herself to say that out loud. Not yet.

"It's just complicated," Maya muttered, her throat tight. "I don't want to mess things up. Not with Ryan, and not... with everything else."

Shelby softened, her teasing tone slipping away. "You mean with Cole."

Maya nodded. "We had plans, Shelby. We were going to graduate and start our lives together. I thought I knew what my future was. I thought I knew who *he* was. And now, I don't know... It's just hard to shake that sometimes."

"I know," Shelby said quietly, reaching over to squeeze Maya's hand. "You guys were together for so long, and it ended... painfully. You're still figuring it out. But that doesn't mean you have to keep punishing yourself. You did nothing wrong."

Maya's heart tightened, the memory of that last night with Cole flickering through her mind like an old movie. The way things had unraveled, so many things said and unsaid between them, hanging in the air like unfinished sentences. She couldn't even pinpoint the exact moment it all fell apart. She just knew that one day she realized that things weren't going to change, and nothing had been the same since.

"And Ryan..." Maya trailed off, struggling to find the right words. "I don't know what's happening there, but I don't want to rekindle that friendship and risk more encounters with Cole. Things were left.... Not the greatest, you know?"

Shelby shifted, leaning forward. "Look, I get it. Ryan is Cole's best friend, and there's history there. But that doesn't mean you have to freeze up every time you two get close. You're allowed to be his friend. Hell, you're allowed to feel something for him beyond that. Cole shouldn't get to stop you from moving on, no matter who that's with."

"I don't even know what's real," Maya said, softer now. "Maybe I just need to accept that things will never be the same between Ryan and I without Cole being hanging over the conversation."

Shelby gave her a soft but pointed look. "And what if they're not. What if it becomes something more? Are you going to keep running away from it?"

Maya shook her head, frustration bubbling to the surface. "I don't know why you think that can happen. That would just be so messy."

"Things are already messy," Shelby said, gently but firmly. "You've got this history with Cole, and now there's Ryan suddenly popping up. I get it, but you can't avoid it forever. That seems to me like a sign that it's something that you should at least consider."

Maya sat in silence, Shelby's words pressing against her chest. She knew Shelby meant well. She had been holding onto the past—onto Cole, and the life they were supposed to have. But life hadn't turned out the way she thought it would. And now, Ryan was back, standing on the edges of her life, and she didn't know what to do with that.

"I just... I don't know if I'm ready," Maya whispered, feeling the weight of it all crashing down on her. "Moving on just feels like it's a backburner concern right now, but moving on with Cole's best friend feels just cruel."

Shelby's expression softened. "You don't have to have all the answers right now. But you also don't have to keep running. Take it slow. See what happens."

Maya nodded, though uncertainty still gnawed at her. "I'll try."

Shelby smiled, a soft nudge of encouragement in her voice. "Good. You deserve to figure this out for you. Cole isn't an innocent party. You need to do what's best for *you*.

Maya leaned back against the couch, her mind swirling with conflicting thoughts. She wasn't sure what the future held, but maybe, just maybe, she could stop running long enough to find out.

Worst case, she got one of her close friends back. What did she have to lose?

Ryan's POV

A week had passed since that moment with Maya in the library, but it was still lodged in Ryan's mind like a splinter he couldn't remove. No matter how hard he tried to push it aside, it lingered, always there at the edges of his thoughts. And now, sitting in his and Cole's apartment for their usual game night, the tension felt like it had its own pulse, heavy and thick between them.

The sound of rapid button presses, and the cheers of virtual crowds filled the room as Ryan focused on the TV, his fingers moving without thinking. His character on the screen was sluggish, though, and he'd already botched a few passes. Cole, on the other hand, was on fire tonight, scoring goals left and right as usual.

Across the room, Alex and Brandon lounged on the couch, sharing a bowl of chips and half-watching the game. Alex, ever the trash-talker, had been throwing jabs all night. "You better pick it up, Ryan," he called out, smirking. "You're getting roasted."

Brandon laughed, grabbing the controller for the next match. "Seriously, dude, where's your head at? You're making Cole look like Ronaldo out there."

Ryan forced a grin, but his heart wasn't in it. He barely registered the light-hearted teasing as Cole scored another goal.

"That's 4-2," Cole said, glancing at Ryan with a look that wasn't just about the game. "You good?"

Ryan shifted in his seat, trying to shake off the feeling that had been gnawing at him all week. "Yeah. Just distracted."

Cole paused the game and handed his controller to Mark, who was leaning forward on the edge of the armchair, always ready to jump in for a match. "Take my spot," Cole said, his tone casual but his eyes sharp as he turned to Ryan.

The room stilled, the air thickening with something more than just competitive banter. Ryan knew what was coming, though he didn't quite know why Cole wanted to do this in front of everyone.

"What's up with you, man?" Cole asked, his gaze narrowing. "You've been off all week."

Mark hesitated, his hand hovering over the buttons, glancing between them. "You guys good?" he asked, his usual grin fading when he sensed the tension.

"Yeah, we're good," Cole answered, but his eyes never left Ryan. "Right?"

Ryan exhaled, trying to keep his tone light. "It's nothing, man. Class load's just been crazy."

Cole's brow furrowed. "Really? You sure about that?"

The room went uncomfortably quiet. Even Alex, always the joker, stayed silent now, sensing the shift in the atmosphere. Brandon threw a glance at Ryan, raising an eyebrow as if to say, *what's going on?*

Ryan knew he couldn't keep dodging this. He tried to ignore the curious stares, especially from Mark, who had clearly picked up on the vibe but was too polite to comment. "Everything's fine," Ryan said, gripping the controller like a lifeline. "Really."

Cole wasn't buying it. "Something's going on, though, isn't it?"

Ryan's heart dropped, and he avoided Cole's gaze, staring at the TV instead. But he could feel the weight of everyone's attention, like they were waiting for something to happen.

He had known this confrontation was coming. Cole had gotten increasingly possessive over Maya towards the end of their relationship, and Ryan had recognized those tendencies making a comeback since running into her again at the store.

Cole wasn't usually one to let things go, but he had done a good job of hiding it for months now. Ryan had almost thought that he was finally starting to accept Maya's choices. Now, he could see that that wasn't the case.

He hated to admit that it irked him, the claim Cole still seemed to think he had over Maya and what she did, who she did it with. Especially since Maya had made no attempt to reach out and Cole had made no attempt to understand why Maya left in the first place, seemingly convinced that she would come back at some point.

Cole leaned forward, lowering his voice but not enough for the others to miss it. "Is this about Maya?"

Ryan froze, his thoughts feeling exposed. The mention of her name sent a ripple through the room. He could almost feel the shift in the guys' posture, subtle but unmistakable, as if they knew this conversation had crossed into dangerous territory.

Brandon sat up straighter, glancing at Alex, who raised his eyebrows but said nothing. Mark shifted uncomfortably in his seat, his fingers tapping restlessly on the controller. No one said a word, but their silence felt louder than any question they could've asked.

"What about her?" Ryan asked, staying as neutral as possible, though he knew the tension was impossible to hide.

Cole shrugged, his eyes locked onto Ryan's. "I don't know. You tell me."

Ryan's heart pounded in his chest. He could feel the pressure building, the tension stretching thin. He thought about the moments with Maya—the grocery store, the library, his beanie, even the way she'd walked away. How could he explain any of that without making it worse? He knew that just the mention of seeing Maya was likely already pushing Cole to this point. Any talk of Ryan intentionally talking to her would only poke the bear.

"She's a friend," Ryan said sharply.

Cole didn't look convinced. "Really? Because you've been weird ever since we ran into her at the store."

Ryan tried to laugh it off, but it came out awkward. "You're reading into things, man. I'm just... tired. You and I both know that's the first time I've seen Maya in months since everything went down, anyway. What else is there to say?"

The room was dead silent now. Even the background noises of the game seemed distant. Alex shot a knowing glance at Brandon, but neither of them spoke, waiting for Cole's response.

Cole leaned back, crossing his arms. "You haven't been yourself, Ryan. And I know it's not just about homework or whatever. So, what is it?"

Ryan could feel everyone's eyes on him now, and the pressure was suffocating. He didn't want to have this conversation, not here, not like this. "I didn't expect that running into her would make me miss having her around," he muttered, hoping that would be enough to drop it.

Cole's question was cold. "*Miss* her?"

Ryan hesitated. "I told you, she's a friend."

Mark cleared his throat awkwardly. "Uh, maybe we should—"

"Stay out of it, Mark," Cole said without looking at him, his eyes still fixed on Ryan.

Ryan swallowed hard, gripping the controller tighter, his knuckles turning white. He could feel the weight of everyone's gaze as if there were pressure building in his head, and the tension in the room was unbearable.

"What do you want me to say? I'm not into her, if that's what you're thinking," Ryan said finally, the words bitter.

Cole snorted, unamused. "Not into her? You're acting like a guy who's into someone."

Ryan clenched his jaw, trying to keep his voice steady. "We've barely spoken."

"But you want to." Cole's challenge was low, almost a threat. The room had gone dead quiet, the usual banter and noise replaced by thick, unspoken tension.

Ryan couldn't deny it. He didn't answer, and that silence was all Cole needed.

Cole stood up, scooping up his phone from the couch. "I thought we understood each other. After everything that happened between you and me, after *she* left."

Ryan's stomach was clenched. All he kept thinking was that he didn't want to talk about this. Not here in front of everyone.

"You need to figure this out," Cole said tightly. "Before it messes everything up."

"Messes *what* up?" Ryan asked, exasperation leaking through. "You're already done. You two aren't together and I've done nothing but respect that, so who cares?"

"I'm going to pretend you didn't just ask the dumbest damn question ever," Cole sneered.

He then walked out of the room without saying another word, leaving the rest of them sitting in a thick, uncomfortable silence. Mark and Brandon exchanged uneasy glances, while Alex let out a low whistle, shaking his head.

"Well," Alex muttered, leaning back. "That got awkward fast."

Ryan stared at the empty doorway, the guilt and tension gnawing at him. He knew things had just gotten a whole lot messier—and it was far from over.

His relationship with Cole was already hanging by a thread based on only two short interactions with Maya. Continuing as her friend would apparently be the end of his friendship with Cole. That thought settled down in his bones uncomfortably as he tried to shift his attention back to the night.

Chapter 4

Ryan's POV

Ryan had replayed that night over and over in his head—like a movie stuck on an endless loop. No matter how hard he tried, he couldn't stop it. The night Cole and Maya finally fell apart.

It had started as any ordinary night—the three of them, together, like always. Maya was in the kitchen, chopping vegetables for a stir-fry, while Cole sat on the couch, scrolling through his phone. Ryan leaned against the counter, sipping a beer, feeling the comfort of their familiar routine.

But that spring evening, something felt different. A tension had settled in, quiet but unmistakable.

Maya had been distant for weeks. And Cole—he was convinced that she was fine. That she would go back to normal like she normally did and go along with what he wanted. They were nearing the halfway point of their master's program, and the future, once so clear, now loomed ahead, full of uncertainty.

They'd been together for four years, always the couple everyone assumed would have it all figured out. But under the surface, Ryan knew things were unraveling.

It was Maya who broke the silence. "I've been looking at jobs," she said casually, her eyes still on her task. "There's an opening in New York that looks perfect."

Ryan glanced at Cole, muscles tightening. He knew what that meant. New York had always been Maya's dream, a city full of possibilities. But Cole? He had different plans. Ryan would have known what was coming even if she hadn't looked at Cole.

Cole's hands stilled, the silence stretching as he put his phone down. "New York?" he asked, a hint of confusion coloring his voice. "I thought we agreed we'd stay here after we graduate. You know, close to my family."

Maya's head snapped up, a frown creasing her brow. "No, you decided that. I didn't agree to anything."

The room seemed to grow colder. Ryan shifted uncomfortably, already sensing where this was headed, but there was no leaving now.

Cole turned toward her, his expression tightening. "We've talked about this, Maya. I want to stay near my family. Settle down, start our lives together."

Maya sighed, rubbing her temples. "I know what you want, Cole. But this is about what we *want. There's nothing wrong with that but I'm not ready to settle down in that way. Not yet."*

Ryan could feel the weight of the conversation pressing down on the room, and he suddenly wished he were anywhere but here. Try as he might, the chair he was sitting in just wasn't enough to buffer him from what was coming.

Cole stood from the couch, folding his arms. "I thought we were on the same page. We've been talking about this for years."

"I don't want to settle down and start a family the second we graduate," Maya said, putting the knife down and pacing the room. "I've worked hard for my degree, for my career. If we start a family right away, I'm the one who has to put everything on hold. Either that, or juggle being a mom and trying to build my career. It's not fair to expect me to do that. You aren't expected to put your own career on pause, you just think I should."

Ryan's throat tightened. He hadn't known it had gotten this deep between them—the plans for a family, the pressures that were suffocating Maya.

Cole stared at her; disbelief etched into his face. "So, what, you don't want a family anymore? We've talked about this for years, *Maya. We were going to buy a house nearby; stay close to everyone we know. You were on board."*

"No, I really wasn't." Maya said, looking away. "I knew that bringing up New York or anywhere that wasn't here only managed to upset you and so I tried not to bring it up." She looked up suddenly, eyes sharp. "That's not fair to me, though, and so lately I have been trying to mention it again, see if you would at least try to have an open mind, but it just seems like you never will. I have tried so long to push past this because I love you but going around in these circles isn't helping either of us, or fair to either of us. To me, it feels like you're pushing me into something where I'm expected to make all the sacrifices. I want to focus on my career, Cole. I want to see what's out there. I've been working toward this for years—just like you have—and now you're asking me to put all of that aside?"

Cole's jaw clenched, his hands flexing at his sides as she spoke. "I'm not asking you to give up your career, Maya. I'm asking you to compromise. We can build a life together here. You know how important family is to me."

Maya shook her head, her frustration growing. "But it's your version of our future. I don't want to just slip into a role because it fits your plan. I want to live my life before I become someone's wife or mother. I shouldn't be the one making all the sacrifices and compromises. But I also understand how important your family is, and I don't want to diminish that or—"

Ryan could see the hurt in Cole's eyes, the disbelief that the girl he'd been with for years—the one he thought he knew—was slipping away.

"So, what are you saying?" Cole asked, the sound raw. "You don't want this? You don't want us?"

Maya hesitated, tears welling in her eyes. "I don't know. I don't feel like I'm being heard or supported, Cole. And I know that I'd be alone trying to balance it all while you worked and left the household stuff on me, which isn't fair, either."

Ryan's chest tightened as he watched the finality in her words wash over Cole, the realization that everything they had built together, everything they had planned, was falling apart.

Cole's voice cracked, desperation leaking through. "We've spent four years building this future together. And now you're telling me it doesn't matter? That I'd be a shitty husband and father?"

Maya looked at him, tears spilling down her cheeks. "It's not that it doesn't matter, Cole, but it's not the only thing that matters. I need time to figure out who I am without everything revolving around your plans. I need to feel like I matter as me and not some piece of your puzzle fulfilling these roles that I'm not ready for. I need to feel like I'm being heard and my thoughts matter and I... I just don't right now. Because I'm more than just a potential wife and mother. You care less about being a husband and father and more about having a wife and children, which isn't the same. I feel like a box you just want to check off anymore."

The silence that followed was unbearable, thick with everything that was left unsaid. Ryan felt like he was intruding on something intensely private, something that was crumbling before his eyes.

Finally, Maya wiped at her face and grabbed her jacket, her movements slow, like she didn't want to make them. She cast a glance at Ryan—brief, filled with guilt, regret—and then she walked out the door, food left forgotten in the kitchen.

The soft click of the door closing behind her felt like the end of something monumental.

Cole didn't move for a long time. He stood there, staring at the spot where Maya had been, his expression unreadable. The room felt suffocating in its silence, as if the air itself had frozen in place.

Ryan stayed rooted to the spot, unsure of what to do, unsure if he should speak.

After what felt like an eternity, Cole finally broke the silence, his voice hoarse and barely above a whisper. "She's gone, isn't she?"

Ryan didn't answer. Because deep down, Cole knew the truth.

Ryan didn't move, didn't dare say anything. Cole was still standing by the couch, his back to Ryan, fists clenched by his side. The only sound was the quiet ticking of the clock in the kitchen.

Seconds felt like hours.

Cole finally exhaled, a shaky breath that told Ryan just how hard he was holding himself together. He knew that feeling—trying to keep everything from crumbling even though the cracks were already too wide to fix.

Ryan cleared his throat, unsure of what to say, if he should say anything at all.

"You knew, didn't you?" Cole's pitch was low, almost a growl suddenly.

Ryan started. He had known something was off, but this? Not the specifics. Not the intensity. "Cole, I didn't—"

"Don't lie to me, man," Cole cut him off, his tone sharper now as he turned around. His eyes were red, but his expression was hard, accusatory. "You're her friend. You spend more time with her than I do lately. You knew something was wrong."

Ryan's heart started beating in staccato. He opened his mouth, but no words came out. He had seen the signs—the distance, the way Maya had been pulling away—but he hadn't realized just how deep it went. He hadn't realized this was the end.

"I didn't know it would go this far," Ryan finally managed in a defeated tone, not sure if he even wanted Cole to hear his reply. "I knew she was stressed, but I thought... I thought you two would work it out."

"Work it out?" Cole let out a cold laugh, wiping a hand across his face. "How? By pretending like none of this mattered? By acting like I was asking for too much? Acting like she hadn't agreed to what was supposed to be our plan? Like she didn't want to get married and start a family with me? Like I hadn't spoken to my family already about getting her a ring?"

Ryan winced. He'd seen Cole ask for a lot, but he'd also seen how much Cole loved Maya, how much he believed in their future together. "It wasn't about you asking for too much," Ryan said carefully, trying to find the right words. "It's just... she needs time, man. She didn't feel heard. She literally just said that."

Cole slammed his palm on the counter, making Ryan flinch. "And what about me? What about what I need? I've been here for her through everything! We had a plan, Ryan. We were gonna build a life together after we graduated. A family. Everything. She just took my future away from me."

Ryan swallowed, unsure how to navigate the conversation without making things worse. Cole's frustration was raw, and it was spilling over.

"I know," Ryan said quietly, leaning against the wall. "But maybe that plan changed for her. She's been focused on her career, on what comes next for her. I don't think she was ready to jump into the future like that."

Cole's face twisted with disbelief. "You're saying I pushed her? Is that it?"

Ryan held up his hands, trying to calm the storm he could see brewing in Cole's eyes. "No, I'm not saying that. But she needs time. You can't force her to be ready for something she's not. She isn't trying to take your future. She's trying to maintain control of her own. But you have a right to your feelings, too. Maybe it's time to show that you do hear her."

Cole stared at him for a long moment, the silence stretching between them, heavy with everything left unsaid. Finally, he dropped his gaze, shoulders slumping like all the fight had drained out of him. "I thought I was giving her everything she wanted. I thought we wanted the same things. I thought we made these decisions together."

Ryan swallowed hard, unsure of how to respond. He didn't want to say the wrong thing, didn't want to pile on the pain that Cole was already drowning in. But the truth was, he didn't think that Cole was hearing her pleas, even now.

"She loves you, Cole," Ryan said softly. "I don't think this is about that. It's about figuring out her life before she can share it with someone else. Maybe you just need to give her space."

Cole shook his head, running a hand through his hair. "I can't believe this. After everything, she just... walks away?"

Ryan felt a knot tightening in his chest, watching his best friend struggle with the loss. But what could he say? There were no easy answers, no quick fixes for this kind of heartbreak.

"I don't know what to tell you, man," Ryan said quietly. "I think she's torn. She wants what she thinks are conflicting things, and it ultimately forced her to choose. You've both been under a lot of pressure."

Cole stood there, his eyes searching Ryan's face as if looking for something—reassurance, maybe. But Ryan had nothing to offer. Not now.

"Space," Cole repeated, almost to himself, the sound hollow. "And what if she doesn't come back?"

Ryan couldn't answer that, so he just stayed silent. That was the one thing he couldn't give Cole—false hope. The reality was, Maya might not come back. And that might be the hardest thing Cole would ever have to accept.

Cole rubbed a hand over his face, finally sinking into one of the chairs by the table, the fight drained out of him. "I thought we had more time. All the time in the world together."

Ryan didn't move, just watched his friend in quiet sympathy. He couldn't fix this, no matter how much he wanted to. And in the back of his mind, the guilt lingered. He had known something was wrong. He just hadn't realized it would come to this.

Cole leaned forward, burying his face in his hands. "What am I supposed to do now?"

Ryan swallowed hard, the weight of the situation settling heavily in the air between them. "I don't know, man. But whatever happens... I've got your back."

Chapter 5

Maya's POV

Maya sat in the small office, her fingers twisting around the strap of her bag as she waited for Professor Whitman to finish looking over her resume. The clock on the wall ticked steadily, and the sound blended with the faint hum of the overhead light. It was strange being here, in this final year. Everything she'd been working toward was so close, and yet... she still didn't feel ready. At least, not in the way she thought she would.

Professor Whitman finally looked up, adjusting her glasses with a warm smile. "You've done excellent work, Maya. Your resume and portfolio are solid, and the internships you've completed will certainly make you a strong candidate for the positions you're considering. You've always had a good sense of direction."

Maya forced a smile, nodding politely. "Thanks, I've tried to stay focused."

Professor Whitman's sharp eyes lingered on her a moment longer, as if sensing the uncertainty bubbling beneath the surface. "But?"

Maya hesitated, exhaling slowly. "But... I'm still not sure what's next. I mean, I know what I *should* be doing—what I've worked for—but the future feels more complicated than I expected."

Professor Whitman leaned back in her chair, clasping her hands together. "That's not uncommon, especially when you're nearing such a big transition. You've been studying for years, and you've got the skills to back it up. But figuring out what path to take is more than just about checking boxes. It's about what you truly want for yourself."

Maya nodded, appreciating the wisdom, though it didn't ease the knot in her chest. "I've been looking at positions in PR and marketing, and New York has some great opportunities. It's always been the dream, you know?"

"New York is ambitious, but it's also full of opportunity," Professor Whitman said, smiling. "You're ready for that challenge."

Maya tried to believe her. She'd been preparing for this for years, diving headfirst into her major and every opportunity that came her way. A career in PR seemed like the perfect fit—she loved working with people, crafting strategies, and making an impact through storytelling. New York was the heart of it all. But every time she imagined herself there, something felt... different. Something she couldn't quite place.

"What's holding you back?" Professor Whitman asked gently.

Maya shifted uncomfortably in her seat, her mind wandering back to the spring, to those long, heated conversations with Cole. She could still see his face, that mix of hurt and disbelief when she'd told him she wasn't ready to settle down. "I guess... part of it is wondering if I'm being selfish. If I'm chasing something that's going to take me away from everything and everyone I've known."

"Selfish?" Professor Whitman raised an eyebrow. "Maya, your career is your own journey. You've worked hard for this, and it's not selfish to prioritize your future. Your life is ultimately yours to choose."

Maya's hands twisted together tightly. "I know, but... it's more than that. I was with someone for a long time, and we had this plan—well, *he* had this plan. To stay local, start a family after we graduated, build a life together." She paused, quieter now. "But it didn't feel like *my* plan. And that's a major part of why we broke up. I couldn't imagine putting everything on hold like that."

Professor Whitman studied her for a moment, the weight of the conversation sinking in. "It sounds like you're torn between what's expected of you and what you want for yourself. That's not uncommon, but it's important to remember that when your choices are made by someone else, the life you end up living is one designed by someone else, and for someone else. It's not wrong of you to want to pave your own future."

Maya nodded, her heart heavy as she thought back to those last few months with Cole. They'd been together for so long—since their undergrad years. It felt natural back then to think about a future with him. But when the time came to talk specifics, things unraveled. Cole wanted a house, to stay close to his family, to start a family of their own as soon as they graduated. It had all felt so set in stone and inevitable.

But when Maya looked at what *she* wanted for her future, all she saw was a career she'd fought so hard for. She'd spent years building her experience, making connections, and carving out a path that was uniquely hers.

The idea of putting that on hold to raise children, to settle into a domestic life so soon—it made her feel like there was a lead weight sinking in her gut despite thinking that she did want children someday. A conversation about when that would happen didn't seem like asking a lot, she thought.

At the same time, New York was starting to feel like a lofty goal now that she was actively trying to make it a reality. There was a lot of competition, and she couldn't help but wonder what life would look like if she wasn't able to land a position there in the first place.

Professor Whitman's advice suddenly broke through her thoughts. "You know, it's okay to want something different than what you thought you wanted a few years ago. People change, and so do their dreams. It sounds to me like you've outgrown a version of your future that no longer fits."

Maya swallowed hard, the truth of that statement hitting her. She *had* outgrown it. The future she'd imagined with Cole wasn't hers anymore. She didn't want to be the woman who put everything on hold just to slip into a role she wasn't ready for. That didn't mean she didn't love the idea of a family—just not right now, not at the expense of everything she'd worked for. She latched on to that thought and nodded slightly.

"You're right," she forced herself to murmur, barely audible. "I guess I just have to figure out how to balance what I want with what feels... like what is expected of me."

Professor Whitman smiled warmly. "You will. And remember, there's no rush. The right opportunities will come. You don't have to have it all figured out today."

Maya felt a sense of calm settle over her, the knot in her chest loosening just a little. She had time—to figure out her next steps, to chase her dreams on her own terms. Cole's plans had been beautiful in their own way, but they weren't hers. And that was okay.

As she left Professor Whitman's office, stepping into the crisp air, Maya wrapped her arms around herself and let her thoughts wander. The path ahead wasn't as clear-cut as she'd once thought, but for the first time in a long time, it felt like hers. And that was a future worth fighting for.

She had agreed to meet Carly after her meeting as Carly had a class ending at about the same time, but before doing so she quickly grabbed her phone and dialed her mom's number.

It rang twice before her mother's warm voice answered. "Maya! Sweetheart, how's my girl?"

Maya smiled despite the tension coiling in her chest. "Hey, Mom. Just finished a meeting with my advisor."

"Oh? How did it go?"

Maya hesitated as she walked toward a quieter part of the building. "Good. She thinks I have strong prospects, especially in New York."

There was a slight pause before her mom answered, and Maya could picture the way she'd purse her lips, thoughtful but careful. "New York. You've been hoping for that for ages."

Maya exhaled slowly. "Yeah."

Another pause. Then—the careful question. "You know I support you no matter what, dear. Do you still think that's what is best for you?"

Maya's hand tightened on the phone. Her mom had always supported her endeavors, but Maya had the impression that she maybe secretly hoped that Maya would find something a little closer to home.

"I do," Maya admitted, keeping her voice neutral. "I don't think there's much for me here. Not career-wise."

Her mom hummed thoughtfully. "Your dad and I just want you to be happy, honey. You know that."

"I know." Maya swallowed. "But?"

A soft sigh. "But New York is... a big step. It's expensive. Competitive. You'd be on your own."

Maya clenched her jaw. "I wouldn't be alone, Mom. Carly might end up there. And... I can handle myself."

"I know you can." Her mother's response was warm, but there was that Maya couldn't ignore. "I just don't want you to feel like you need to prove something, sweetie. You've always been independent, but sometimes I wonder if you push yourself so hard because you think you have to."

Maya stopped walking, her hand automatically moving to push her hair behind her ear. *Because you think you have to.*

She wasn't sure why, but those words hit a nerve.

Was that what she was doing? Chasing New York because she wanted it? Or because she was terrified of being stuck—of settling into a life that was too mundane?

Her mother continued softly. "I just don't want you to feel like you have to run, Maya."

Maya forced a small laugh, trying to shake the tension in her chest. "I'm not running, Mom."

Her mom was quiet for a moment, then sighed. "Okay. I trust you. Just promise me one thing?"

Maya swallowed. "What's that?"

"Don't be so focused on the future that you forget to enjoy right now. Sometimes we get so caught up in what's next that we don't appreciate what's in front of us."

Maya nodded, even though her mom couldn't see her. "I'll try."

"Good." Her mother said before changing direction. "Now, tell me—how's Carly? And Shelby? Have you all been taking care of yourselves?"

Maya exhaled, letting the conversation shift, but her mom's words lingered in the back of her mind.

I just don't want you to feel like you have to run.

As she hung up a few minutes later, she suddenly spied Carly sitting on a bench across the quad from her.

"You're the best." Maya told Carly genuinely, taking the coffee being offered as she sat on the bench. Taking a sip of the warm coffee, she groaned in appreciation.

"I know." Carly replied playfully. "Class let out a tad early, and I needed a pick me up. How was your meeting?"

"Good, I think." Maya responded carefully, "I just need to keep doing what I have been, but Whitman seems positive about me getting a decent position, even in New York, so that's a relief."

Her thoughts swirled in the cool air as Carly responded. She'd just begun to loosen the knot of worries tangled inside her when, out of nowhere, a thought she'd been pushing down for days crept in.

Ryan.

She clenched her jaw, trying to shove it back into the corner of her mind. It was ridiculous. She hadn't been thinking about him—*didn't want* to think about him—but after running into him again, the memory of his easy smile and the way he'd made her feel that day at the coffee shop had been harder to shake than she'd like to admit. She could almost hear him teasing her, asking her what she was doing here.

The thought made her pulse quicken, and Maya scolded herself internally. She had no idea if he'd end up there—he was still figuring things out himself. And even if he did move to New York, what did that mean? Nothing.

Nothing.

And yet, she didn't quite want to admit to herself that her feelings for Ryan might be shifting. Her mom's words rang in her ears one more time about enjoying the now and not solely focusing on the future. Maybe spending that time with Ryan could lead to both now and later being brighter.

But he was Cole's best friend. He wouldn't do that to Cole. She shoved the thoughts and feelings as far down as she could and turned her attention back to Carly forcing herself to focus.

Ryan had no place in this conversation, no place in her future. At least, not in the way her mind had started to wander.

Carly nudged her, not letting her off that easily for spacing out. "What's that look for?"

Maya blinked, startled by the question. "What? Oh, nothing. Just... thinking about everything."

Carly gave her a knowing look but didn't push for once. "Well, I'm glad things are looking good. That's one less worry!"

Maya smiled, grateful Carly hadn't pressed further before changing the subject and passing along her mom's well wishes and encouragement for Carly.

She wasn't ready to unpack the confusion that came with Ryan, especially when there were already enough unresolved pieces of her life to handle. But as much as she tried to push him away, the thought lingered, a whisper of what-ifs in the back of her mind.

Instead, she and Carly chatted as they walked to their next classes, in adjoining buildings, thankfully, about Carly's plans and what she wanted to see happen in the next few months.

Maya curled up on the couch, her laptop balanced on her legs as she scrolled through job listings. The golden autumn sun streamed through the window, casting long shadows across the floor. She could hear Cole in the kitchen, the rhythmic clatter of dishes as he put them away.

Her heart picked up when she saw an opening at a top New York firm—competitive, but exactly the kind of opportunity she'd been dreaming of. She clicked on it, skimming the requirements.

"I swear, these applications all blur together after a while," she called out.

Cole emerged from the kitchen, wiping his hands on a dish towel. "You still looking at marketing jobs?"

"Yeah." She hesitated, then tapped the screen. "This one looks perfect. It's a PR agency in New York—really high-profile."

Cole didn't even glance at her laptop. Instead, he dropped onto the couch beside her, pulling her feet into his lap like he always did. "New York, huh?" he said, his tone light, almost amused. "You're still on that?"

Maya blinked. Still on that?

She frowned slightly, sitting up straighter. "Uh... yeah. Of course, I am. I've been talking about New York since last year."

Cole made a noncommittal sound, rubbing small circles against her ankle with his thumb. "I just figured you'd end up somewhere around here. You know, stay close. LA, maybe."

Maya's core tightened in anticipation of his next words as she asked, "Why would you figure that?"

Cole shrugged, eyes still on the TV. "I don't know. You love it here. And most of your connections are in California."

Her fingers hovered over the keyboard, her focus on the job posting forgotten. "I like it here," she said carefully. "But I want to try something different. You knew that."

Cole let out a short laugh, shaking his head. "Babe, come on. You always say stuff like that, but when have you ever actually wanted to leave? You'd miss it too much."

Maya's chest tightened. "I told you I was serious about New York," she said, softer this time, like she was trying to remind him.

Cole finally looked at her, his expression shifting slightly, like he wasn't sure why she was pressing the issue. "Okay, so you get a job in New York," he said. "Then what?"

Maya hesitated. "What do you mean?"

He leaned back against the couch, one arm draped casually along the backrest. "I mean, what's the plan, Maya? You go to New York for a few years, then we settle down here? Or are we supposed to do long-distance?"

The air in the room changed.

Maya stared at him, feeling something in her sink. "I... don't know."

Cole huffed a small laugh, like he thought the answer was obvious. "Maya, my family is here. My job is here. I figured we'd get a place after graduation, you know? Start our life together. Married in a couple years, maybe kids soon after that..." He grinned like he was picturing it, like it was already set in stone.

Maya felt her hands go cold.

Married. Kids. A place here.

He hadn't even considered another option. Hadn't even thought to ask what her version of the future looked like. Hadn't considered the sacrifices she would have to make for this version of the future to become a reality.

Her question came out quietly. "Have you even looked at jobs outside of California?"

Cole blinked, caught off guard by the question. "What?"

"You're applying for jobs, right?" she pressed. "Have you even considered anything in New York?"

Cole let out a breath, shaking his head like she was missing the point. "Why would I? My life is here, Maya. Our *life is here."*

And just like that, she saw it—the life he had planned, the one where she fit neatly into the space beside him.

She had told him about New York. She had told him for months. But he had never actually heard her.

Because in his mind, it had never been a real possibility.

Maya swallowed, forcing a small nod. "Right. Of course."

Cole smiled, satisfied, like the conversation was over. He leaned in, pressing a kiss to her temple before reaching for the TV remote.

Maya didn't say anything else. She just let him.

But later that night, lying awake in the dark, she stared at the ceiling, unable to shake the feeling that something had just shifted.

Because for the first time, she realized—maybe she couldn't have both.

Chapter 6

Maya's POV

Maya tried to hurry her steps as she made her way across the quad. She was already later than she had planned and the campus career fair was buzzing with energy. Booths lined the student center, representatives from various companies handing out brochures, and students huddled in small clusters, nervously eyeing each opportunity.

Maya tugged her coat tighter around her shoulders as the cool breeze followed her inside, shaking off the early fall chill.

Shelby and Carly were already there, the latter talking to a recruiter from some big firm, but Maya had decided to check out other tables first. It wasn't her scene, and she was trying not to let the swarm of professional chatter overwhelm her.

Her plan after graduation still felt unclear. Sure, she had ideas and a general desire to be in New York, but nothing concrete. Professor Whitman had given her some guidance, but seeing all these companies laid out made her realize how much she still had to figure out.

Her eyes darted to different company names, trying to decide what might be a good fit for her even with the application process being so competitive.

As she wandered past a booth for financial firm, she caught sight of a familiar face. *Ryan.*

She paused for a moment. She hadn't expected to see him again so soon after their last encounter. He looked focused, listening intently to the recruiter, a folder tucked under his arm. His dark hair had grown slightly longer since she'd last noticed, and despite the tension of the past few weeks, she couldn't help but feel that slight pang of familiarity.

Without thinking, she approached him, weaving through the crowd.

"Hey," she called, keeping her voice light.

Ryan turned, his face registering surprise for a split second before a soft smile spread across his lips. "Maya. I didn't expect to see you here."

She shrugged. "Figured I'd see what companies were out. Get a sense of what's next."

Ryan nodded. "Yeah, same. Though, I'm mostly looking at corporate finance firms. Risk management, I think." He paused, his eyes scanning hers. "It's good to see you again, Maya."

There was a sincerity in his face that caught her off guard. She hadn't realized how much she'd missed him until now. "Yeah, it's been... a while," she said.

They started walking together, Ryan thanking the man he had been speaking with. As they made their way to another section of booths, the ease of their conversation was surprising—almost as if no time had passed, despite the tumultuous history between them.

Ryan glanced over at her, his expression softer now. "I've missed you, you know. Since... everything."

Maya's steps faltered for a moment. The unspoken weight of "everything" hung between them: her breakup with Cole, the months of silence that followed, and the awkwardness that crept in whenever she saw Ryan. She managed a small nod. "Yeah, I've missed you too."

Before either of them could say more, they heard another familiar voice. "Ryan, man! I didn't think you'd make it."

Cole. Not again.

Maya's heart sank as she turned to see him approaching, trying yet again to suppress the memories that the sight of him dredged up. He was smiling, but the sight of him stirred a confusing mix of emotions. His usually confident gait was slightly stiffer, as though he wasn't quite as at ease as he appeared. His grin was tight, his eyes flicking quickly between Maya and Ryan.

"You guys catching up?" he asked.

Ryan shifted, his eyes darting between her and Cole. "Just talking about the fair," he replied, forcing a smile. "What about you? Find anything interesting?"

Cole shrugged. "A few firms. You know, engineering companies are always looking for software developers." He paused, his gaze sharp as it flickered between them. "Figured you'd be busy with finance stuff."

"I am," Ryan said, his tone neutral. "Just looking around."

"Ah, I got here a little late. Work," Cole said, casually glancing at Maya. His smile wavered slightly, but he kept up the easygoing façade. "Didn't expect to see you either, Maya. How's it going?"

Maya swallowed the awkwardness building in her chest. "Just... seeing what options there are," she said, trying to sound light.

The air felt thick with unsaid things, with history that was still too raw.

Ryan shifted beside her, the tension between him and Cole palpable. Maya had never noticed before how Cole's presence seemed to unsettle Ryan, but it suddenly seemed crystal clear.

"Hey, I was thinking... maybe we could grab coffee sometime? Catch up, you know? It's been a while," Cole said calmly, but with an undercurrent of something deeper.

Maya's pulse quickened. Cole asking her for coffee felt like a test, a way to pull her back into his orbit. She hesitated, glancing briefly at Ryan, who was staring at the floor, hands shoved deep into his pockets.

"Uh, yeah... maybe," Maya responded, unsure if she should commit. It would be easy to fall into the past with Cole, but did she really want to? Was coffee with him just prolonging something she needed to let go of?

Ryan cleared his throat, lifting his gaze back to her. "It's been really good to see you, Maya. I'm glad we ran into each other." His words were soft, but the sincerity was palpable.

Maya gave him a small smile. "Yeah, me too. It's been... nice."

Cole's smile faltered slightly, sensing the subtle shift in the air. He looked between them, his jaw tightening ever so slightly. "Well, let me know about that coffee," he said, a little sharper than before.

"Right," Maya said, feeling torn with if it was even a good idea. She glanced at Ryan, almost involuntarily, and saw a flash of something in his expression. It almost looked like... guilt? Jealousy? It was gone before she could pinpoint more, though.

Cole gave a short nod and turned, disappearing back into the crowd. Ryan stood there, his expression now unreadable, before he glanced down at his watch. "I should probably check out a few more places," he said, his tone more distant now.

Maya nodded, suddenly feeling the tension suffocating again. "Oh, okay, I'll... see you around."

"Yeah," Ryan murmured, his eyes lingering on hers for just a second longer before he walked away, his arm brushing hers as he passed. Watching him disappear into the crowd, Maya exhaled, her mind swirling with questions.

The more she thought about meeting Cole for coffee, the more she realized it wasn't clarity she was searching for. What was it she really wanted? Closure, or something else?

And Ryan... she had always liked Ryan and appreciated that he was a good guy, but it almost felt like those feelings were shifting into something she wasn't used to feeling. She felt almost protective of Ryan and didn't want him to feel bad about just speaking to her because of Cole.

She shook her head, wandering through the maze of booths, letting herself get lost in the various companies and opportunities. The thought of coffee with Cole still lingered in her mind, but she pushed it aside. She wasn't ready to deal with that yet.

Stopping at a booth for a digital marketing firm, Maya scanned their information, her thoughts distracted until she heard a familiar voice.

"Hey, Maya! You checking this one out too?"

Maya turned to see Carly approaching, her bright smile making her stand out in the crowd. Carly had always been one of those people whose energy radiated outward, contagious and full of life. Her curly hair was tied back today, and she had the effortless confidence of someone who knew exactly where she was headed. Maya admired that about her.

"Yeah, I figured I'd see what they're about," Maya said, smiling back. "It's a competitive field, so I want to keep my options open."

"Same," Carly said, reaching for a brochure from the table. "I'm really hoping to get into something more creative. Digital strategy is where the fun is."

Maya nodded. Carly was a social media whiz, always thinking outside the box when it came to branding and marketing. They had a few classes together over the years and had become fast friends. Carly always had an eye for trends. She was driven but never let herself get overwhelmed by the competition, a balancing act Maya struggled with.

"How's the job hunt going?" Maya asked.

"Pretty good, actually. I've been talking to a couple of smaller agencies that seem promising. I just want to be somewhere I can make an impact, you know?" Carly's excitement dimmed slightly, her brow furrowing. "But I need to find a company that's okay with my whole 'I might want to freelance' vibe."

Maya chuckled. "Freelance? Really?"

"Yeah," Carly nodded. "I like the idea of working with a variety of clients. Plus, more flexibility." She paused, a mischievous smile tugging at her lips. "Also, in case I decide to move back to Portland. Rachel's out there, and... well, I miss her."

Maya arched a brow. "Rachel? I didn't know you two were still in touch."

Carly shrugged, looking a little sheepish. "We weren't for a while after she moved. But we reconnected a few months ago. It's been nice. We're taking things slow, but who knows, maybe it'll lead to something more again." She laughed lightly. "Guess I should've known I couldn't stay away from her forever."

Maya smiled warmly. "Good for you," she replied. "It sounds like things are falling into place."

"I hope so," Carly murmured, her eyes bright with hope. "Anyway, enough about me. What about you? I noticed you and Ryan looking cozy."

Maya grimaced. "We were just catching up."

"Uh-huh," Carly said, giving her a teasing look. "Well, let me know how that coffee with Cole goes, too. Sounds like you've got a busy social calendar."

Maya groaned. "You heard that? Have you been stalking me?" She laughed softly, trying to take the edge out of her voice.

"You wish!" Carly smiled.

They chatted some more, moving between booths until Maya spotted Shelby standing near the exit. She waved them over, her auburn hair catching the light as she looked at them expectantly. Shelby, ever the pragmatic one, had a grounded energy that contrasted with Carly's spark. She was sharp, detail-oriented, and had a clear path ahead in her field of pediatric medicine.

"Finally! I thought you two were never going to get out of there," Shelby teased as they approached.

"Blame Maya. She got distracted," Carly quipped.

"Of course she did." Shelby smirked before pulling them both into a quick hug. "Anyway, I'm starving. You two ready for lunch?"

Maya nodded. "More than ready."

As they left the fair behind, the tension from earlier slowly began to ease. They strolled down the tree-lined path toward a café off-campus, the chilly air nipping at their cheeks. Shelby, always the planner, was already talking about their post-graduation plans.

"Honestly, I just want to lock down a solid residency before summer," Shelby said as they walked. "Preferably one of my top choices, obviously, but as long as I can get in somewhere, I can always move around later once I'm established."

"You will," Carly said confidently. "You're too good at what you do."

"Thanks," Shelby replied, glancing at Maya. "What about you? Any luck at the fair?"

Maya shrugged. "It was... okay. I'm just trying to figure out where I really want to go after graduation. It's all so competitive and overwhelming. I want to be in New York, but I really need to start narrowing down my choices for firms."

Shelby nodded. "You'll find it. Just don't let anyone—" her eyes twinkled mischievously, "—Ryan, for example—distract you from what's important."

Maya laughed, though the mention of Ryan tugged at her thoughts again. She was grateful to have friends who supported her, but as they headed toward the café, she couldn't shake the memory of Ryan's words or the way he had looked at her.

Her mind drifted for a moment—Ryan's career might take him to New York. He hadn't mentioned it today, but she remembered hearing it in passing. The thought made her smile.

She quickly pushed it aside. She couldn't allow herself to go there. Not with Cole's best friend.

They found a cozy corner table at the café, the warm, earthy scent of coffee and fresh pastries filling the air. The windows fogged slightly from the chill outside, and Maya was grateful for the comforting atmosphere. As soon as they sat down, Shelby, being Shelby, flagged down the server and ordered.

"I'll have the veggie panini with a chai latte," she said smoothly. "What about you two?"

Maya glanced at the menu but barely registered the words. "Just a tomato soup and grilled cheese," she said absentmindedly, still lost in thought.

Carly added, "Cobb salad and a black coffee for me, please."

Once the server left, Carly leaned back, stretching her arms out. "God, I needed this. That fair was more intense than I expected."

"I know, right?" Shelby said. "It's always such a frenzy. But hey, it's nice to see options. Hospitals seem to be popping up left and right. They're even talking about offering signing bonuses for entry-levels at some places. That's unheard of."

"That's amazing," Maya said with a soft smile, though her heart wasn't fully in it. She glanced at her friends, the comfort of their presence calming her slightly. But the weight of everything that had happened earlier was still heavy in her chest.

Carly noticed immediately, narrowing her eyes at Maya. "Okay, spill. You're being weirdly quiet, and that's not like you."

Shelby raised an eyebrow, clearly in agreement. "Yeah, something's up. I can feel it."

Maya sighed, glancing between them, and then gave in. "It's... well, Cole asked me to coffee."

Shelby's eyes widened. "Cole? Seriously?"

Carly leaned forward, her interest piqued. "Wow, that's a curveball. What did you say?"

"I didn't give him an answer," Maya admitted, watching their reactions carefully. "I don't know why, but I'm thinking about going... maybe it'll give me some closure."

Shelby and Carly exchanged a glance before Shelby spoke. "Do you *really* think it'll bring closure? Or is Cole trying to pull you back under his control?"

Maya hesitated. "I don't know. It felt weird, like... he wasn't over it. Or us, I guess. There's this... tension, I guess. And not just with me. Between him and Ryan."

Carly leaned in closer. "Tension? With Ryan? I knew something was off when I saw you three together at the fair. What's going on?"

Maya looked down at her hands, fidgeting with the edge of her napkin. "It's hard to explain, but ever since the breakup... things have been weird. I hadn't talked to Cole in months, and then today he just showed up and acted like... like we were just old friends that happened to not talk for a while or something. And Ryan—" she paused, unsure of how much she wanted to say about Ryan. "—well, I don't think he's comfortable with it. There's something... tense between them that I can't put my finger on."

Shelby crossed her arms, her expression serious now. "Maya, you know how Cole can be. If there's tension, he's probably the one feeding it. You guys broke up for a reason, remember? And if he's trying to reel you back in... you need to be careful. He can be a master manipulator when he wants to be."

"I know," Maya said quietly, barely above a whisper. "Things just seem so different now."

Carly tilted her head, curiosity flickering in her eyes. "Different how?"

Maya shifted uncomfortably. "I don't know exactly. Just... different. On one hand, I feel like Ryan and I could pick up being friends from where we left off, but I also feel oddly protective of him. I don't want to cause issues for him. And at the same time, I know I could never pick anything up again with Cole and when he showed up today... it just got weird."

Shelby leaned forward, her tone more cautious now. "You aren't responsible for their friendship. If they stop being friends, that's not on you, no matter the reason."

Maya didn't answer right away. She wasn't sure how to. Her feelings for Ryan were knotted up in her history with Cole, in the memories of their group dynamics, and in the guilt that tugged at her whenever she thought too long about it.

"I... don't know," she finally said. "I never thought about any of Cole's friends like anything more than just friends, but... I'm not ready to think about that. There's too much going on right now to be sidetracked with maybes. And I couldn't start something with someone so close to Cole anyway."

Carly raised an eyebrow. "Sounds like a lot to unpack."

Shelby's voice softened. "Maya, just be careful. You've got so much going for you, and your career is just starting to take off. Don't let Cole—or Ryan—complicate that for you."

Maya nodded, appreciating the concern. "I know. I should just let things go before they become complicated, huh?"

The server came back with their food, and for a moment, they all fell into a comfortable silence as they ate. The warmth of the café, the familiar chatter of her friends, and the steady hum of the world around them were a welcome relief from the chaos of her thoughts.

Maya leaned back in her chair, toying with her straw. "But enough about me. What about you guys? Carly, you mentioned talking to Rachel again. How's that going?"

Carly glanced up from her food, her expression shifting slightly. "Yeah... I've been talking to her. It's... complicated, as always," she admitted, her fingers tracing the edge of her napkin. "She's still in

Portland, so we're doing the long-distance thing for now. I'm looking into some freelancing up there, but... I don't know. It's a big move, and we all know how well things went last time."

Shelby raised an eyebrow, leaning in. "Last time? You mean when she moved away without really discussing her plans with you before and it blew up?"

Carly nodded, a rueful smile tugging at her lips. "Yep. That's the one. We thought we could handle the distance, but it got messy real quick. Now, I'm thinking about giving it another shot...," she added with a laugh, though the nervousness was hard to miss.

Maya gave her a sympathetic smile. "Maybe this time it'll be different. You've both grown, right?"

Carly shrugged, her eyes focused on her salad. "Maybe. But the distance is still the same, and I don't know if I'm ready to pack up my life here and just... follow her to Portland. Especially when I'm just getting a foothold here."

Shelby reached over and squeezed Carly's arm gently. "Whatever happens, we've got your back. And Portland's not that far, really. You could totally make it work if you decide you want to."

Carly looked up and gave her a grateful smile. "Thanks, Shelbs. I know. It's just... a lot to think about."

Maya glanced at Shelby. "And you? Anything new in the romance department?"

Shelby grinned sheepishly. "Well, I've been seeing someone... casually. No labels or anything serious. I'm just too focused on my classes and residency applications to get into anything deep right now. Dating feels like just another thing to juggle."

Maya raised an eyebrow. "Casually? That's a surprise coming from you."

Shelby laughed. "I know, right? But it's been fun—no pressure, no expectations. It works for now. Besides, I'm practically living at the hospital, so the last thing I need is a relationship that demands too much."

Carly teased, "Sounds like you found the perfect arrangement, then."

Shelby chuckled. "Exactly. It's nothing complicated. And after the last guy who spent the entire date talking about himself, this feels refreshing."

Maya smiled at their banter, appreciating the normalcy of the conversation, though her thoughts kept drifting back to the tension between Cole and Ryan. Seeing them both again had stirred up things she hadn't expected to deal with. But for now, her friends' lives were a welcome topic.

Chapter 7

Ryan's POV

Ryan slouched on the couch half-watching the game on TV. Cole sat next to him, but his mind seemed elsewhere—fidgeting, eyes distant. Ryan could feel the tension between them, thicker than usual, and it wasn't about the game.

"Hey," Cole muttered, breaking the silence. "Maya still hasn't gotten back to me about meeting for coffee."

Ryan stilled, trying not to react to this news. Ten months. That's how long it had been since Cole and Maya broke up, but it didn't feel like it to him. The memories of those awkward weeks after the breakup, the lingering looks between Maya and Cole, still hung in the air. And now, Cole wanted to reopen old wounds, but Ryan wasn't sure how he felt. About Maya and Cole.... Or just Maya in general.

"Yeah?" Ryan tried to keep his voice steady, focusing on the game, though his mind was spinning. He had no business feeling like this—jealous, of all things. Cole was his best friend, and Maya was... complicated.

Cole leaned forward, rubbing the back of his neck. "I don't know, man. I thought maybe things could... I don't know, get back to how they were. Maybe we just needed space, you know? But she hasn't even responded."

Ryan fought to keep his expression unreadable. The idea of Cole and Maya back together... it twisted something in his gut. He had no right to feel this way, but he couldn't shake the pang of jealousy that tightened in his chest. The thought of Maya going back to Cole, slipping into the life they'd once planned, left him feeling unsettled in a way he didn't want to explain.

"You think that's a good idea?" Ryan asked carefully, trying to sound casual as he sat up straighter on the couch. "I mean... maybe she's moved on."

Cole's eyes flicked toward him, narrowing slightly. "You don't think we could work things out?"

Ryan hesitated, unsure how to navigate this conversation. "I think... you know how Maya is. She doesn't rush into things but once she has her mind made up...."

The silence that followed felt heavy, and Ryan shifted uncomfortably. He didn't want to be the guy who encouraged Cole to keep pursuing something if it wasn't right, but he also didn't want to see Maya pulled back into the past. He also, selfishly, found himself not wanting them to get back together.

Cole shrugged. "Yeah, I guess. But it's just... I can't stop thinking about her."

Ryan didn't reply immediately, the feeling of jealousy creeping up again. Cole wasn't wrong—Maya was hard to get out of your head. But Ryan had spent the last few months pushing those thoughts aside, doing everything he could to not let his feelings get in the way of their friendship.

He and Cole might be best friends, but he had considered Maya a friend for a long time now, too, and that had been hard enough to deal with in the midst of Cole's pain but now that he had been talking to Maya again, he didn't think he would be able to cut her out of his life so easily this time.

But maybe.... Maybe this would be the closure that Cole would need to move on and for Maya to make it clear that that chapter was closed and she was looking for something other than what Cole could give her.

After all, Maya had been right all those months ago. Cole was the type of guy who expected the woman to take care of the home and the kids and have dinner on the table every night. That kind of expectation didn't leave room for her to be able to build her career in the way Ryan knew she wanted to.

She really was more than a potential wife or mother. Maya's a woman and Cole had really taken her for granted in a way that Ryan couldn't unsee now that he was looking in hindsight. Considering that Cole hadn't ever been the introspective type, Ryan doubted much had changed with his opinions there.

Ryan was trying hard not to see her as exactly that himself, though. The difference was that Ryan had always anticipated his wife being his partner and equal, not his maid. He couldn't imagine being a hands-off father. If he made the decision to have kids, then he would be there for them no matter what. That much he knew.

Once the game ended, Cole stood up, stretching. "Anyway, I'll figure it out. Just needed to get that off my chest."

Ryan nodded, watching Cole walk into the kitchen. As soon as he was out of sight, Ryan pulled out his phone. He hesitated for a moment before typing out a message to Maya.

Ryan: Hey, about Cole asking you to coffee. I think maybe he might have meant more with that than meets the eye, but it might give you both some closure... and maybe help him move on too.

He stared at the screen for a moment, debating whether to hit send. His thumb hovered, his mind still stuck on the nagging feeling of jealousy, the idea of Cole and Maya reconnecting. It wasn't his place to feel this way, but it was impossible to deny.

Finally, he hit send and tossed his phone aside as if it had burned him. His mind raced, wondering what Maya would do—and why, despite his best efforts, he couldn't quite shake the idea of her.

As he sat on the couch, his eyes flicked back to his phone every few seconds. He had no idea why he was so nervous. It was just a message. He'd sent hundreds of texts to Maya over the years, but this felt different. Maybe it was because of Cole. Or maybe it was because, after all this time, he was suddenly finding himself yearning to see her and talk to her, laughing and joking without all the baggage.

His phone buzzed, and he instinctively picked it up.

Maya: Hey… Yeah, I've been meaning to respond. I don't know if it's a good idea, though. Feels like it could get messy again.

Ryan exhaled, staring at her words. He could hear her in his head—thoughtful, careful. Always weighing her options.

Ryan: Yeah, I get that. I don't think he's moved on. Maybe he's got an ulterior motive, but maybe it'll help both of you.

He debated adding more but settled on keeping it simple. He didn't want to sound pushy. Maya didn't reply right away, and for a moment, he thought she was done with the conversation. But then, another message appeared.

Maya: You really think I need closure? Or are you just trying to get rid of me?

Ryan's lips quirked into a grin. He could practically see her raising an eyebrow, that playful edge to her words. It was a side of Maya he hadn't seen in a while, and it made him relax.

Ryan: If I wanted to get rid of you, I'd have found a way by now. Trust me.

Maya: Oh really? You think you're that clever, huh?

Ryan leaned back, his fingers hovering over the keyboard as he considered how to respond.

Ryan: Clever enough to know you're hard to shake off. You always come back around. Not that that's a bad thing.

There was a longer pause this time, and Ryan felt a flicker of nerves again. Did he push too far? Was he flirting with her? Did he want to keep going?

When her response came, he couldn't help a bark of laughter.

Maya: Well, I guess I'm just irresistible then.

He typed quickly, barely thinking before hitting send.

Ryan: Always have been.

The words hung there, and for a moment, he wondered if he'd crossed a line. But then, another message came.

Maya: Careful, Ryan. You're starting to sound like you miss me.

He bit his lip, his heart doing a weird little flip in his chest. His thumbs hovered over the screen before he responded.

Ryan: Maybe I do. You ever think about that?

There. It was out in the open now, and he wasn't sure how she'd take it. The seconds ticked by, and his mind raced, imagining every possible reaction.

Finally, her reply came through.

Maya: Guess I'll have to keep coming around then, won't I?

He smiled at his phone, a sense of relief and something else—something warmer—settling in his chest.

Ryan: Guess so. But for the record... even if you don't get coffee with Cole, it won't change anything, and you can still talk to me whenever.

Ryan: And if you're around campus, maybe I'll see you at the coffee shop. I'll be there too—sometimes it's good to catch up with old friends, right?

He hit send and waited. The tension between them, even through the phone, was palpable. But this time, it didn't feel as heavy as it used to. It felt like something else entirely.

Maya: Maybe I'll have to start stopping there more often 😊

Ryan smiled, not realizing that Cole had been in the doorway watching his face for several moments, jaw tense and arms crossed.

Maya's POV

Maya walked into the coffee shop, the rich aroma of roasted beans greeting her as she made her way to the counter. She'd decided to stop by for a quick caffeine fix before her day got underway and that decision definitely had nothing to do with talking to Ryan the night before. The place was bustling with students, but she managed to find a cozy spot by the window.

After ordering a large cappuccino and a muffin, she settled down with her book, sipping her coffee and losing herself in the pages. Time seemed to slip away until she glanced at her watch and realized she had to head to class soon.

Packing up her things, she grabbed her remaining coffee and headed toward the door. As she pushed it open, her mind was already on the lecture she had to attend, and she didn't notice the figure coming through the door at the same time.

In an instant, they collided. Her coffee cup wobbled dangerously, and she felt a jolt as she nearly lost her balance. But before she could react, a firm hand grasped her arm, steadying her and preventing the coffee from spilling. The electricity in his touch sent a sudden, unexpected tingle through her arm.

Maya looked up, her eyes meeting Ryan's. He was standing there, his expression a mix of surprise and concern, as his hand lingered on her arm. His touch was warm and reassuring, and the contact sent a shiver down her spine.

"Whoa, careful there," Ryan said, a small, relieved grin appearing on his face. "We really need to stop running into each other like this."

Maya laughed nervously, her head spinning from the collision and the lingering touch. "Yeah, it's becoming a something of a habit, isn't it?"

Ryan adjusted the coffee cup carefully, making sure it was back in her grip. His fingers brushed against hers for a moment, and she felt a jolt of electricity at the contact. "I'm glad I was here to catch you," he said softly. "It's nice to see you. Again."

Maya felt a blush creeping up her cheeks. She tried to sound casual, though the flutter in her chest betrayed her. "I guess we're just destined to bump into each other."

Ryan chuckled, the sound warm and inviting. "Maybe it's a sign we should catch up more often."

Maya hesitated, glancing around to make sure she wasn't running late. "I'd like that," she said finally. "But right now, I've got to run. I don't want to be late for class."

"Same here," Ryan said, stepping aside to let her pass. "But maybe we can set up a time to actually sit down and talk. For real."

Maya nodded, feeling a small thrill of anticipation. "That sounds good. Text me?"

As she turned to leave, she glanced back at Ryan. The softness of their brief contact lingered, making her smile as she waved at him. "Have a good day, Ryan."

"You too, Maya," he replied, watching her walk away with a hopeful smile.

As Maya exited the coffee shop, she felt a flutter in her throat. She turned back one last time to give Ryan a parting smile and wave, the feeling of their touch still fresh in her mind.

She then hurried to class and sat down, the professor's lecture a distant hum as she tried to focus on the notes in front of her. Her mind, however, was elsewhere. Thoughts of Ryan and their unexpected encounters kept intruding, a reminder of the unfinished business between them.

Ryan's warm touch and his hopeful smile lingered in her mind. She wondered about the possibility of rekindling their connection, but the thought of revisiting her past with Cole was still a heavy weight on her shoulders. Her encounter with Ryan had only intensified her need to resolve things with Cole.

As the professor's words faded into the background, Maya pulled out her phone and checked her messages. She'd been avoiding Cole's request for coffee, unsure of how to handle the situation. But the conversation with Ryan, coupled with her own desire for closure, had made up her mind.

She needed to face Cole and close that chapter of her life properly. She couldn't move forward with Ryan, or really anyone, until she had dealt with her past. Cole needed to move on so she could preserve the new beginnings she hoped for with Ryan, should that path ever open.

Maya took a deep breath, her fingers moving decisively over the screen as she typed out a message to Cole.

Maya: Hey Cole, I've been thinking about it and I think meeting up for coffee is fine. Maybe it's time we talk things through and find some closure. Let me know when you're free.

She hit send and stared at the message, feeling a mix of relief and anxiety. This was a step she had to take for her own peace of mind and to ensure that she could move forward without any lingering doubts.

The crack of something hitting the floor in the front of the room brought her back to the present, and she tried to refocus on the lecture, but her thoughts kept drifting. She was determined to handle this meeting with Cole well, so she could finally lay to rest the past that had been haunting her.

With a renewed sense of purpose, Maya resolved to meet Cole, hoping that this step would allow her to move on and embrace whatever future she might have with Ryan. The thought of finally closing that chapter gave her a small sense of peace as she prepared to face the rest of her day.

Cole: Tomorrow? I have class til 2.

Maya: Sounds good. I'll see you then.

Chapter 8

Maya's POV

Maya arrived at the cozy café and spotted Cole waiting for her at a secluded corner booth. The intimate setting was meant to offer privacy, but the air between them felt heavy with uncertainty. As she approached, Cole stood and pulled out a chair for her.

"Hey, Maya," he greeted with a tentative smile, trying to keep the mood light. "Thanks for meeting up."

Maya offered a small smile in return as she took a seat. "Hi, Cole. I thought we should talk. It's probably long overdue, really."

They both settled in, and Cole looked at her with a mixture of hope and determination. "How have you been?"

Maya smiled faintly, "I'm okay. You?"

Cole leaned forward over the table, jumping right into the part of the conversation that had Maya clenching her hands together under the table to stay composed. "I've been thinking a lot about us lately. I know things ended abruptly, but I miss what we had. I was wondering if maybe we could work things out."

Maya sighed, her heart aching. "Cole, I'm here because I need closure. I need to move forward, and I don't think revisiting the past will help with that. I think you need to move on, too."

Cole's expression grew earnest. "Maya, I understand that you're hurt, but we had something special. Maybe we could find a way to make it work. I know I'm asking a lot, but I really think we could with another chance."

Maya's gaze softened with sadness. "It's not that simple. There were real issues, and they haven't just gone away. I need to focus on what's best for me, which doesn't include going back to the way things were."

Cole's face tightened, his frustration beginning to show. "I just don't get it. We can work through this. You won't even give me a chance to show you why staying in California is for the best!"

Maya was already shaking her head. "Cole, you still aren't hearing me." She started but he cut her off.

"Is it because you've already moved on?"

Maya's heart dropped as she jerked back, feeling as though she had been slapped. "What do you mean?"

Cole leaned in, dropping to a more intense tone. "I've seen you around. You've been with Ryan. Is that why you're shutting me out? Are you with him now? You leave me and start shacking up with my best friend? Is this supposed to be some sick twisted revenge?"

She was shaking her head again, beyond confused. "What? That's not true at all. I don't know what you're talking about!"

Cole's anger flared, his volume rising. "Don't lie to me. I've seen the way you two interact. I know you're in love with him. Is that why you're pushing me away? Because you're with him?"

Maya felt a surge of discomfort and fear. "Cole, that's not true. I'm not with Ryan. This is about me moving forward with my life and career, not about being with someone else."

Cole's face darkened with rage. "So, you're saying you weren't seeing him while we were together? Because it sure looked like you were."

Before Maya could respond, Cole's hand shot out and grabbed her arm tightly, his grip painful. She winced as he squeezed, his hand a vise. "Cole, please—let go!" she pleaded, her body trembling. "You're hurting me."

Cole's eyes flashed with anger as he held her arm firmly. "If you were with him while we were still together, then you owe me an explanation. Why should I believe you now?"

Maya's voice cracked with distress as she repeated herself. "Please, Cole. You're hurting me. Let go!"

He hesitated, his grip loosening slightly but not completely releasing her. His eyes were still filled with a mix of anger and disbelief. "I just want to understand why."

Maya jerked her arm free, rubbing the tender skin. Her pulse roared in her ears and tears of frustration and fear welled up in her eyes. "I don't know what you're talking about, but I can't do this right now. I need to go."

Cole watched her stand; frustration etched on his face. "Maya, don't walk away from me!"

Ignoring his outburst, Maya hurried out of the café and started walking anywhere to get away from Cole. She was almost sobbing at that point, and debated calling Shelby for a ride, but she had never seen Cole behave in such a manner before. She was suddenly afraid he would hurt Shelby and, in that moment, made a split-second decision. Crossing the street, she dialed Ryan's number with shaking hands. Her breath hitched in another sob as she spoke.

"Ryan, it's Maya. I need your help. Cole's... he's angry and accused us of having an affair when we met for coffee. I've never seen him like that. I don't know what to do. I don't want him to do something, but—"

Ryan's voice was immediate and concerned. "I'm on my way. Just hang tight."

Ryan arrived at the café moments later, his expression a mix of worry and determination. He quickly spotted Maya walking down the road, looking distressed. Without hesitation, he stopped and approached her.

"Maya," Ryan said softly, his presence strong but comforting. "Let's get you out of here."

Maya nodded, gratefully accepting his support. As Ryan guided her towards his car, Cole's eyes locked onto them from down the road. The sight of Maya with Ryan only seemed to anger Cole further.

Ryan gently placed his hand on Maya's lower back as he opened the passenger side door for her and helped her in before running around to get in the car himself. Maya felt the heat of his touch even after he pulled away from the curb.

In the car, Maya took a deep breath, feeling a mixture of relief and lingering unease. "Thank you, Ryan. I didn't know what to do. I don't know why he thinks we—""

Ryan glanced at her, his concern evident. "It's okay. We'll figure this out. Just breathe. Don't worry about me, I can take care of myself, you know."

Maya managed to smile and tried to wipe her face off, the tension from her encounter with Cole still clinging to her. She didn't say much more after he picked her up, but her thoughts were running wild. Ryan's presence beside her was comforting, yet the emotions swirling inside her were anything but calm.

"I'm sorry I called you. I'm sure Cole isn't happy about it and it'll probably complicate things for you. I was going to call Shelby, but I didn't want them to get into it and she get hurt." Maya confessed finally.

"I wasn't far when you called," Ryan responded, pulling into a quiet side street near a small park. He turned the car off and looked over at her, concern softening his gaze. "I'm glad you did. Are you okay?"

She let out a shaky breath, her fingers tracing the part of her arm now bruised through her jacket sleeve. "I don't know. I didn't expect it to go like that." She paused, struggling to put the jumbled mess of feelings into words. "Cole's... not himself. I've never seen him that angry before."

Ryan's jaw tightened, and she could see his knuckles whitening as he gripped the steering wheel. "I'm sorry he put you through that."

Maya pulled her sleeve up slightly and glanced at the mark on her arm, feeling as though someone had thrown a bucket of ice on her, even now out of Cole's presence. "He's convinced I was seeing you while we were still together. That's what really set him off."

She saw Ryan shift slightly in his seat, his expression hardening, but he didn't speak. He looked uncomfortable, and she wondered what was going through his mind. The thought of him worrying about Cole made her chest tighten in a way she decided not to think about.

"He's been getting worked up for a while now," Ryan finally said, quieter than before. "He asked me about you the other day, but I didn't realize it had gotten this bad."

Maya nodded, the weight of everything sinking deeper into her chest. She could still hear Cole's accusations in her mind, sharp and accusing. And worst of all, she felt that all-too-familiar pang—how he still didn't really see her, still expected her to fall in line with his plans.

"He just doesn't understand that it's over," she whispered, more to herself than to Ryan. "It's like he still wants me to follow his plans, like nothing ever happened."

Ryan turned to face her fully, his eyes searching hers with quiet intensity. "What about you?" he asked, cautious now. "What do *you* want?"

The question caught her off guard. It shouldn't have, but it did. She'd been so consumed by Cole's expectations and inability to actually listen to her, that Ryan actively asking her what she wanted caught her off guard. The question hit her harder than she expected.

"I want to move on," she admitted, barely above a whisper. "It's been so long and he still doesn't hear me. I want to figure out my life, my career... I thought I needed closure from him, but maybe it's time for me to realize he isn't going to hear me. He isn't going to change his mind for me. And New York is competitive enough that I can't have the added distraction of a relationship that will never go anywhere with him."

Ryan's gaze didn't waver, his expression soft yet steady. "You deserve that, Maya. You shouldn't have to keep putting up with not being seen or heard."

Maya's heart squeezed at his words. There was something about the way Ryan spoke—how he always made her feel like her choices mattered, like *she* mattered. And at that moment, it was like a weight lifted, even if just a little.

"I don't know what I'd be doing without you," she said, the words escaping her before she had time to second-guess them.

Ryan's lips curved into a soft smile, his eyes lighting up slightly. "You're stronger than you think."

A quiet ease spread through her at his response. She looked down at her hands, her fingers still grazing the faint bruise on her arm and suddenly felt the urge to distance herself from the chaos that had consumed her life over the past few months.

"I think I need to skip class," she said with a small, half-hearted laugh. "I just... I need a break."

Ryan didn't hesitate, nodding toward the park outside. "Let's go for a walk."

They got out of the car and began walking through the park, the quiet of the afternoon breeze wrapping around them like a comforting blanket. The rustling of the leaves overhead and the distant sound of birds filled the space between them, giving Maya time to breathe, time to let her mind settle.

As they strolled along the path, she felt the tension in her chest slowly unwind. It was easier, being with Ryan like this. Easier to just exist without all the pressure.

"I thought I might need to talk to him one more time to actually be able to say what I need to say," she finally said, hesitant as the words spilled out. "But after what happened today... I need to close that chapter for good and move on. Maybe he finally will, too. Graduation is just too close and we're going in different directions; I really don't think I'll see him again afterwards."

Ryan didn't respond immediately, and when she glanced over at him, she noticed the slight shift in his expression—a flicker of something she couldn't quite read. Relief, perhaps?

"If that's what you think you need," he said finally, his tone calm, though she sensed the tension beneath it. "Just... be careful. I'm not sure how he'll react to being completely iced out."

Maya looked at him, her heart sinking slightly at the concern in his voice. "I will. I just don't want us to lose our friendship again because of all this. Or your friendship with Cole, either. I know you're close."

Ryan's gaze softened as he looked down at her gently. "You won't lose me this time. I promise. You never should have in the first place. I'll have to see how things go with Cole...."

The way he reassured her, the certainty in his tone, made her heart flutter unexpectedly. She let out a quiet laugh, trying to shake off the intensity of the moment. "We really need to stop running into each other like this," she teased, her eyes meeting his with a playful glint.

Ryan chuckled, the tension easing slightly from his posture. "Maybe we're just meant to."

Her breath caught at his words, a gentle calm spreading through her chest. The playful back-and-forth felt natural, but there was something else there, too, something deeper simmering beneath the surface. She wasn't sure what to say, so she let the moment hang between them, both caught in that fragile space between familiarity and something new.

As they continued walking, side by side, Maya felt lighter. But even as they moved through the park, she couldn't shake the feeling that things between her and Ryan were changing. Maybe today's events were the tipping point they had needed to see the truth.

She grabbed onto his arm as they walked, and he didn't shake her off or tell her not to. And for the first time in a long time, that possibility of things changing didn't scare her.

Chapter 9

Ryan's POV

Ryan walked beside Maya, hands stuffed in his jacket pockets, trying to keep things light as they strolled through the park. He talked about anything and everything that came to mind—the weather, a new café opening nearby, the squirrels darting across the path—anything to keep her mind off what had happened with Cole.

But inside, he was boiling.

Though he hadn't been there to witness it, an image of Cole grabbing Maya's arm, hurting her like that, flashed through his mind, and Ryan's fists clenched tighter in his pockets. He kept stealing glances at her, remembering the slight bruise on her arm when she had pulled up her sleeve in the car, the tension still lingering in her posture.

He wanted to hit something—no, *someone.* How could Cole do that? He'd never imagined his best friend could cross a line like that, but seeing the aftermath made it impossible to ignore.

And then there was that accusation.

An affair? Ryan felt sick at the thought of Cole's words. He'd barely been able to control his anger when Maya told him. How could Cole seriously believe that? Ryan had been nothing but respectful when Maya and Cole were together. He'd been their friend, their *mutual* friend—never once crossing any of their boundaries. Yet somehow, in Cole's mind, he and Maya had been sneaking around. Betraying him.

It was ridiculous. But worse than that, it was *dangerous.* Dangerous for Maya, for what it meant about Cole's state of mind. And Ryan had unwittingly played a role in getting them to sit down, providing exactly this opportunity for Cole to hurt her. He shoved his self-loathing away for the moment.

Ryan's eyes shifted to her again, her expression still guarded despite their conversation. He hated that Cole had shaken her like this. She didn't deserve any of it. Not the accusations, not the pressure to get back together, and definitely not the physical aggression. He had been surprised and thrilled to see her calling but immediately shifted to terrified when he heard her fear. He had never heard or seen her lose her composure like that before and it made some deep part of his soul react in a visceral way.

Ryan's knee jerk reaction to Maya cutting off Cole again was to leap for joy. She didn't have to meet him again. It wasn't worth it. But he held back, forcing himself to stay calm. She wasn't asking for his permission or opinion, and he wasn't about to appear to me making decisions for her like Cole had tried to.

Instead, he had carefully tried to walk a line between supporting her decisions but not forcing his own opinions upon her about seeing that bastard again.

He couldn't shake the gnawing feeling that this wasn't over, that Cole wasn't going to just let go. Maya didn't deserve to go through this again—Cole pulling her back into his life, twisting the knife deeper with every accusation and expectation.

And if Cole hurt her again...

Ryan's anger surged up again, but he swallowed it down. He couldn't show her how upset he was—she had enough to deal with already. But the thought of Cole continuing to mess with her, of pulling her into that toxic spiral, made Ryan's blood boil.

Maya still wanting to be his friend eased a deep fear he hadn't even realized had materialized until she said she didn't want to lose him again.

Her eyes had softened, and something in her expression made his pulse quicken. She still didn't realize how much she meant to him, how important that promise to stay was. He decided that he couldn't bear the thought of losing her again, of letting things slip away like they had before.

They walked in silence for a while, the weight of everything they weren't saying hanging between them. He glanced at her every now and then, trying to read her mood. She seemed a little lighter, at least on the surface.

When she grabbed his arm to walk, he thought his heart would combust. He was still avoiding the thoughts of what this meant about his true feelings for Maya but knew subconsciously that he was fighting a losing battle on that front. It took everything in him to not pull her even closer. He wanted to let her take the lead with this.

But Ryan couldn't stop the swirl of emotions inside him—anger at Cole, fear for Maya, confusion about why things were unraveling the way they were. While the thought had never actively crossed his mind during Maya and Cole's relationship, Ryan knew that he had always been much closer with Maya than any of his other friend's girlfriends but just had chalked it up to Cole being his best friend and being closer to Cole meant being closer to Maya.

Ryan couldn't shake the feeling that things were changing. The connection between them, the ease with which they talked—it was different now, more charged, more alive. He couldn't tell if she felt it too, but something told him she did. After all, why would she grab his arm to walk if she didn't? It felt too intimate to be a casual gesture.

That thought alone scared him a little. This was his best friend's ex. He wasn't allowed to have these feelings for her. He was supposed to be on Cole's side no matter what. The fact was, though, that Cole's behavior and attitude were increasingly alarming Ryan, and he couldn't let that slide. Being best friends didn't mean allowing them to do whatever they want and never disagreeing. It also didn't mean that his emotions were dictated by who Cole thought he should be with.

At the same time, Ryan wasn't sure that they were best friends anymore. Not only did Cole put his hand on Maya, which was unforgivable, but Ryan's own feelings that had now started to surface for Maya would inevitably cause tension, too. No matter how off-limits Maya was supposed to be.

And if he did pursue Maya, he knew that would be the end of any chance of reconciling with Cole down the line, as well. The thought of losing Cole's friendship didn't seem so bad in comparison to standing by and allowing him to act this way, though.

As they neared the car, Maya brushed her hand against his arm, a light touch that sent a jolt through him. He felt his heart speed up, the tingling sensation lingering long after her fingers had pulled away.

"You sure you're okay?" he asked, softer now.

As they stopped by the passenger door, Maya pulled away and turned to Ryan, her smile soft but filled with gratitude. "I'll be fine. Thanks, Ryan. For everything. I know I said it already, but I truly don't know what I'd do without you."

Before he could respond, she stepped forward and wrapped her arms around him in a hug. Ryan could feel her body heat through his jacket, and for a moment, he let himself relax into it, closing his eyes as the familiar scent of her hair drifted up to him. His arms tightened around her, just slightly, for a moment longer than they should have.

It was more than a friendly hug—he could feel it, the way her fingers curled into his jacket, how her body pressed against his for just a second too long before she finally pulled away. When she did, her cheeks were faintly flushed, and she gave him a shy smile as she stepped back, tucking her hair behind her ear.

"I'll drive you home," Ryan said, clearing his throat to cover the sudden feeling bubbling up. He motioned toward the door, and Maya nodded, her gaze lingering on him before getting into the car.

The drive was quiet, neither of them saying much, but the silence felt different now—comfortable, as though the air between them had shifted in the last hour or two. Ryan kept glancing at her, catching the way she looked out the window, lost in thought. He wondered if she felt it too, that spark, that undeniable attraction that he was suddenly starting to notice in everything that she did.

When they reached her place, Maya turned to him, her expression grateful but also a little hesitant, as if there was more she wanted to say. But instead, she just smiled softly and said, "I'll see you soon?"

"Yeah," Ryan replied quieter than usual. "You will."

She opened the door and stepped out, giving him one last look before heading inside. Ryan stayed in the car for a moment, gripping the steering wheel as he tried to steady his thoughts. His emotions were all over the place—relief that she was okay, anger at Cole, and something else... something he didn't quite want to put into words yet.

As soon as she disappeared into the house, Ryan put the car into gear and headed home. He wasn't done for the night. There was one more conversation he needed to have.

It was time to confront Cole.

Ryan pulled into the driveway; his jaw clenched tight as he parked the car. The weight of the evening still pressed heavily on his shoulders. He had tried to calm himself during the drive, but the moment he saw Cole's car in the driveway, the simmering anger inside him reignited.

He slammed the car door shut and walked toward the house, each step heavy with purpose. Cole had decided he wasn't going to let Maya go, but neither was Ryan going to let this behavior off the hook.

As soon as he stepped inside, Ryan found Cole in the living room, sitting on the couch, his posture stiff and rigid. The tension in the air was palpable, a dark cloud hanging over the space between them. Cole's head snapped up when Ryan entered, and the anger in his eyes was unmistakable. It was clear that Cole had been stewing for hours.

"So," Cole spat out, his voice dripping with sarcasm, "did you have fun with Maya tonight?"

Ryan's fists clenched at his sides. He hadn't even been there for ten seconds, and already Cole was throwing accusations. "I picked her up, Cole. She was scared—because of *you*."

"Because of me?" Cole shot to his feet, his eyes blazing. "Nothing would have happened if she wasn't lying to my face! I know she's been seeing you. You two have been messing around this entire time!"

Ryan took a step closer, his head spinning with implications of the words being thrown at him. "We didn't have an affair, Cole. Not then and we aren't sleeping together now, either."

"Bullshit!" Cole shouted; his fists balled at his sides. "She's lying, Ryan, and you are, too. You think I didn't notice the way you've been looking at her? You think I didn't see it back then? You were always around, always there, pretending to be my friend while you waited for your chance."

Ryan's blood boiled. "I never betrayed you," he said through gritted teeth, choosing to ignore that Cole's accusations weren't even cohesive. "You and Maya fell apart all on your own. That's on you, man, not me."

Cole took a step forward, getting in Ryan's face now. "Don't you fucking pretend you didn't want this, didn't want her. You probably had your hands all over her just now."

"Stop!" Ryan snapped, his voice loud and sharp. He shoved down the memory of her touch and pushed Cole back, his anger rising to a dangerous level. "She called me because she was *terrified*. Do you even care about that? You *hurt* her, man. You grabbed her. You *bruised* her."

Cole's face twisted into a sneer, his retort lowering to a deadly tone. "You think you're better than me? Huh? You think you're her knight in shining armor, swooping in to save the day? That she'll fall in love with you now?"

Ryan's breath came in short, heavy bursts as he tried to keep control, but his fists were shaking. He was done tiptoeing around Cole's emotions regarding this breakup. "This isn't about being better. This is about you hurting her. It's over between you and her and it's time that you accept that."

Cole's eyes darkened, and without warning, he shoved Ryan hard, sending him stumbling back a few steps. "I'm not letting her go."

Ryan saw red. He lunged forward, shoving Cole back with equal force. "You already lost her, Cole. You're just too blind to see it. She left you and she isn't coming back. And you know what's messed up? I told her that I thought it might be good for you two to sit down, and *this* is your reaction to that? Your temper and possessiveness will be the downfall of any relationship you have if you don't figure your shit out."

And that was all it took.

Cole swung first, his fist connecting with Ryan's jaw, splitting his lip open. The taste of blood filled Ryan's mouth, but the pain barely registered. Without thinking, he retaliated, his fist slamming into Cole's face. A sickening crack echoed through the room as Cole's eye swelled instantly, the skin bruising before either of them could catch their breath.

Cole staggered back, clutching his face, but he wasn't done. He charged at Ryan again, tackling him onto the floor. They grappled, fists flying, each one fueled by anger and years of friendship breaking apart.

"You fucking snake," Cole spat, pinning Ryan down for a moment. "You've wanted this all along."

Ryan, his lip bleeding and heart in overdrive, shoved Cole off him and stood up, breathing heavily. "I didn't want this!" he yelled. "You did this to yourself! I never asked to care about her!"

Cole wiped blood from his nose, glaring up at Ryan. "She'll never want you. You know that, right? She'll always come back to me."

Ryan's chest heaved with the force of his emotions, but he didn't strike again. He just shook his head, looking at Cole with something close to pity. "Like she did tonight? Calling you when she was scared? Like you aren't the person who made her feel that way? She doesn't love you anymore. And, honestly, I don't know if you ever loved her. You need to move on."

Cole, clutching his bruised eye, scoffed bitterly. "You can think what you want."

"Cole, you have to realize that if you've been with other people since the breakup that she has that same right, with whomever *she* chooses." Ryan tried to appeal to his logic one last time. After all, Cole hadn't exactly been chaste these last months.

"What I do and who I do it with has nothing to do with this." Cole landed a punch in Ryan's abdomen, making him double over.

As he caught his breath, he saw Cole's fist flying again, so he scrambled to the side and pushed Cole into the dining table. "You need to get over yourself." Ryan panted. "She doesn't want you and whenever she moves on and with who is none of your business anymore. Maybe she already has."

Ryan turned away, walking toward the door, his lip still bleeding and his body aching from the fight. As he reached for the handle, he paused, glancing back at Cole. "And if you ever lay a hand on her again, I'll make sure it's the last time you use it."

With that, Ryan left, slamming the door behind him, the sound echoing through the silence that followed.

Carly's POV

Carly hummed quietly to herself as she sorted through a stack of homework on her desk, trying to ignore the mess that had accumulated in the past week. Her phone buzzed, interrupting her concentration. Glancing at the screen, she raised an eyebrow—Ryan. It wasn't unusual for him to reach out, but the late hour was. She swiped to answer.

"Hey," she greeted, tapping the screen to put it on speakerphone. "What's up?"

"Uh... are you home?" Ryan's voice was low, rough—definitely off.

"Yeah, why? What's going on?" She heard the hesitation in his breath and knew something was wrong.

"I... could I come over? I just need—" He paused, almost as if he didn't know how to ask. "I need to talk to someone."

Carly frowned, her worry spiking. Ryan wasn't the type to just show up out of the blue unless something was seriously wrong. "Yeah, of course. Come on over. Are you far?"

"I'm close," he muttered. "Be there in ten."

She hung up, her mind racing. This wasn't just about blowing off steam; it was more than that. She finished cleaning the papers off her desk and grabbed a glass of water, pacing around her tiny kitchen as she waited.

When the knock came, it was quicker than she expected. Carly opened the door to find Ryan standing there, his face a mess—lip split, dried blood on his chin, and a bruise forming near his cheekbone. Her eyes widened.

"What the hell happened to you?"

Ryan shrugged, but his usual cool exterior cracked. "Got into it with Cole."

"Cole did this?" Carly stepped aside, letting him in. "You guys don't fight like this. What's going on?"

Ryan walked into her living room, sinking onto the couch with a tired groan. "We've had a... thing. You know. Tension."

"A thing?" Carly shot him an incredulous look as she grabbed the first-aid kit from her bathroom. "This isn't a 'thing.' This is a full-on brawl."

Ryan ran a hand through his hair, wincing as it grazed a bruise near his temple. Carly returned with the kit and sat down beside him. She leaned in, gently dabbing his lip with an antiseptic wipe, her touch firm but careful.

"Alright, talk," she said, focused on cleaning him up. "You can't just show up with a busted face and not give me the details."

Ryan was silent for a moment, his jaw tight. "He thinks something's going on with me and Maya. Like... that something was going on when they were still together."

Carly's hand stilled for a second, her eyes snapping to his. "Was there?"

"Of course not." He replied sharply. "You know me. I wouldn't do that to either of them. And Maya never would have betrayed Cole like that."

"I know." She admitted before going back to cleaning his face, her movements softer now. "So, why does Cole think that?"

Ryan sighed, leaning back against the couch. "I don't know. He's been off since the breakup, and when Maya called me today—after Cole lost it on her—things escalated."

Carly's eyebrows shot up. "Cole lost it on her?"

"He grabbed her arm. Hurt her. *Bruised her.* She called me because she didn't know what to do. Didn't want you or Shelby to be involved if things escalated more, I suppose." His fists clenched at the memory. "I picked her up from campus, and Cole saw her get in the car. Apparently, that confirmed his suspicions of us messing around last year and still now, I guess."

Carly let out a low whistle, now understanding why the situation had gotten out of control. "Damn... no wonder he's pissed. But he's wrong, right?"

Ryan exhaled, the weight of the question pressing on him. "There's nothing between us, not like that. But I can't say that I don't think about her. I mean... we've been hanging out more since the semester started. I... missed her."

Carly paused, gauging his reaction as she gently pressed a bandage to his lip. "So... there's something."

Ryan closed his eyes, rubbing the back of his neck. "I don't know. There could maybe be something, but I can't let it happen. Not with Cole..."

Carly sighed, packing up the first-aid kit. "Ryan, Cole's projecting his insecurities onto you. Maybe you have feelings for her, maybe you don't, but either way, his actions are not about you. It's about him not being able to let go. And you... you need to figure out what you really want."

Ryan glanced over at her, eyes troubled. "And what if I can't? Or worse, what if I just blow everything up and Maya gets hurt even more? She deserves better than that."

She gave him a soft, knowing smile. "You won't let that happen. Just don't avoid it. Talk to Maya, figure things out, and if it's time to let her in... then do it."

Ryan's phone buzzed, and Carly glanced at the screen. "Is that Maya?"

He checked the message and sighed. "Yeah. Just checking in after everything today."

Carly smirked. "You better answer her before she thinks you've ghosted her. And Ryan?"

"Yeah?"

"Maybe you shouldn't hold back... so you don't lose the chance. Maya's a grown woman. She can handle making her own choices."

Ryan shot her a small smile, appreciation in his eyes as he opened the text to reply. Carly leaned back against the couch, watching him type with a quiet, knowing grin. She had known Ryan a long time, and she could tell that he truly cared about Maya—she just hoped he wouldn't wait too long to act on it.

She also knew Ryan well enough to recognize the tension in his shoulders, the way he glanced at the door, as if dreading what came next.

"You're not planning to go back there tonight, are you?" Carly asked gently, folding her arms.

Ryan paused, his thumb hovering over his phone screen before he sighed, rubbing his temples. "No. I can't go back tonight. Not after... everything."

Carly nodded, her expression softening. "Good. I wasn't going to let you, anyway. You're staying here."

Ryan blinked, looking up at her with surprise. "I don't want to—"

"—you're not intruding," Carly interrupted, waving off his concern. "I've got a couch, blankets, pillows... the works. Besides, I'd rather you stay than go deal with more Cole drama tonight. I might even have some shorts for you. And a towel.... If you need to shower." She glanced at his blood splattered shirt under his jacket.

Ryan opened his mouth to protest again, but Carly gave him a pointed look. "Don't even try to argue. You need a place to crash, and this is it. No questions."

Ryan chuckled softly, giving in. "Alright, alright. Thanks, Carly."

"Don't mention it," she said with a grin. "Just be prepared for my obnoxiously early work schedule. I'm up before the sun."

Ryan leaned back into the couch, the weight of the day seeming to catch up to him. She knew he hated imposing on anyone, but going back to the apartment with Cole wasn't an option right now. Not after their fight with emotions still running so high.

"Think I'll crash here tonight," Ryan finally muttered, more to himself than anyone.

Carly smirked, already tossing him shorts, a pillow and blanket. "Smart choice, Mr. Finance. You need some sleep before you do something else crazy."

Ryan caught the pillow, shaking his head as he stood up to get cleaned up. "Guess I owe you one."

"Oh, you owe me more than that. But we'll hash that out later."

"Deal," Ryan replied.

As Carly headed to her bedroom, she threw one last look over her shoulder. "And Ryan? You'll figure it out. Just... don't keep running from whatever feelings you might have. Face them head-on."

Ryan didn't reply, but she heard the shower start a little later and hoped he was really listening.

Chapter 10

Ryan's POV

The morning sun was already warming up the pavement as Ryan walked alongside Mark and Emily toward campus. The still crisp breeze did little to cool the heavy weight in his chest, though. His mind was still buzzing from the events of the night before. The argument with Cole felt like a bad dream, and he was still trying to make sense of it.

"Dude, you look like crap," Mark said, nudging him with his elbow, snapping Ryan out of his thoughts. "How are you holding up?"

Ryan forced a chuckle, though it felt hollow. "Thanks for the vote of confidence, man." He ran a hand through his hair, glancing down at the sidewalk. "It was a rough night."

Emily, walking just a step behind them, chimed in softly. "What happened with Cole? Mark told me it wasn't great."

Ryan sighed, shoving his hands into his pockets. "We got into it. He thinks there's something going on between me and Maya. It blew up fast. I tried to explain, but he wouldn't hear me out."

Mark glanced at him, frowning. "That sucks. You guys have been tight forever. I'm surprised he'd go there."

"Yeah, well, he's been different ever since the breakup," Ryan muttered. "I thought things were going to settle and really thought he was moving on, but it's like he's suddenly stuck on this idea that I've been waiting around for her. Or took her, I guess, and have been hiding it from him all this time."

Emily stepped closer, her brow furrowed in concern. "And have you developed feelings?"

Ryan's teeth clenched at the question, his mind flashing back to the way Cole had spat those words at him. He shook his head, though it didn't feel as certain as he wanted it to. "No? I mean... I don't know. I mean I dated Brittany for a year. I just haven't wanted to date again since then. Seeing Maya yesterday, I don't know... it just triggered some instinct to protect her, I think."

Mark's eyebrows arched as the trio stopped at a crosswalk. "Do you have a 'why'? What's kept you single?"

Ryan hesitated. He hadn't really thought about it before. He'd just been... focused on other things. School, life, everything else. But as Mark's question hung in the air, the nagging thought crept in: *Why hadn't he pursued a new relationship?*

"I guess I've just been busy," he said finally. "Not that it would have stopped me if I met the right person, but I also don't think Cole would have taken me being in a new relationship great, either. I'm sure he would have seen it as me rubbing it in his face. Maya and I have always been close but pursuing her would be so wrong.... Right?"

Mark grunted. "Yeah, he probably would be pissed no matter what you did. Seems like a no-win situation with his mindset."

Emily watched him closely, her expression unreadable. "But now that Cole's brought it up... does it make you wonder?"

Ryan's chest tightened, and he avoided her gaze. It did make him wonder, but he didn't want to admit it. If he started questioning everything now, it would just make things worse. Cole was already pissed beyond reason—if Ryan started doubting himself too, it would only feed into his accusations.

"I don't know," Ryan muttered, kicking at a loose pebble on the ground. "I just want things to go back to normal. I don't want to lose my best friend over something like this. He's really the one to blame for how things ended with Maya, but he doesn't want to hear that. He's a hypocrite, anyway. He's been sleeping around whenever he wants since they broke up. Even if Maya and I were something now, it's not wrong for her to move on."

Mark sighed, glancing at Emily before turning back to Ryan. "You might have to face the fact that things won't go back to normal, man. Not unless you and Cole talk it out and come to some agreement, which isn't likely. You can't just hope it'll blow over and I also really don't see him being okay with it if you and Maya did start a relationship."

"I tried talking to him last night," Ryan reiterated, frustration bubbling up again. "But every time I open my mouth, he just assumes I'm lying."

Emily pursed her lips for a moment before speaking. "Maybe give him some space? Let things cool off, and when you try again, he might be more willing to listen."

Ryan nodded, though he wasn't sure if space was going to help. It felt like there was a wall between him and Cole now, and every attempt to break through only made things worse.

They rounded a corner, the sounds of campus life growing louder as they neared the main quad. Ryan's thoughts, however, remained tangled in the aftermath of the fight. Cole had been more than just angry—he'd been hurt. And even though Ryan knew he hadn't intentionally done anything wrong, part of him still felt guilty.

Maybe he should've been more careful, should've distanced himself from Maya more. But then again, Maya was his friend too. And he hadn't seen her in months after their breakup. If it weren't for his inattention and literally running into her at the store, he's not sure they would have reconnected at all.

He couldn't just continue to push her away because of Cole's jealousy. Not now that the semester had started and their paths had crossed again. Not ever again.

"I just don't know how to fix it," Ryan admitted. "I feel like I'm caught between them, and no matter what I do, it'll be a betrayal to someone."

Mark gave him a sympathetic look. "You're not betraying anyone, man. You're trying to be good friends to both. If Cole can't see that right now, then it's on him to figure it out."

Emily nodded. "You shouldn't have to choose between them. But maybe it's worth thinking about where your own feelings are in all of this. If one relationship isn't healthy anymore, it might be time to let that one go, painful as it might be."

Ryan swallowed hard. His feelings? He had been consciously avoiding those all morning. Everything had spiraled so fast—Cole's outbursts, the tension with Maya, the lingering guilt he couldn't shake. He really didn't want to end his friendship with Cole, either, but the way things were going it seemed like it wouldn't be up to him. Even if it hadn't been Maya on the receiving end, Cole's behavior was inexcusable.

They walked in silence for a few minutes, the weight of Emily's words settling over him. Was this really about Cole's accusations? Or was it about something Ryan hadn't let himself admit? He had never thought of Maya that way. He has been with Brittany for a good chunk of that time, but had he suppressed these feelings that were finally surfacing?

As they reached the main entrance to the lecture hall, Ryan slowed his steps, staring at the building as though it held the answers to everything he was grappling with. But it didn't.

"Thanks, guys," he finally responded.

Mark clapped him on the shoulder. "Anytime, man. We're here for you."

Emily smiled softly. "Don't be too hard on yourself, Ryan. Just take things one step at a time."

He nodded, but even as they parted ways and headed inside, Ryan couldn't shake the feeling that he really would have to make a choice and that it would be a painful one.

Maya's POV

Maya walked into class alongside Carly, the cold air from outside still clinging to them. Carly was animatedly discussing her recent projects, her enthusiasm a welcome distraction from Maya's troubled thoughts.

"...so, Rachel and I were brainstorming some ideas for her new gallery show," Carly was saying. "It's been some back-and-forth with our different schedules, but we're making it work. I have been hesitant about moving there after graduation, but I think I'm really leaning in that direction now. I think I might have even lined up some freelance work that I might get to start soon."

"That sounds exciting," Maya replied, trying to stay upbeat. "It's good to hear you're working things out with Rachel, even from a distance."

"Yeah, we're doing our best," Carly said, smiling. "It's been a challenge, but she's really been great about it. I'm just trying to balance everything right now. It can really get to be so overwhelming."

They entered the classroom, and Maya slid off her jacket. She distractedly focused on Carly, who seemed to sense her unease, but didn't pry, allowing Maya space while continuing to talk about her upcoming projects.

"So, what about you? How's everything going with the final semester?" Carly asked, glancing at Maya with genuine concern.

Maya forced a smile. "It's been... a lot, honestly. Trying to figure out post-graduation plans and dealing with all of the planning and scheduling that goes with that. I hate the uncertainty. I haven't finished applications and haven't heard back from those I have submitted, so everything feels like it's in limbo."

As Carly pulled off her own jacket, she suddenly noticed the bruise on Maya's forearm, dark against her skin. Carly's eyes widened slightly, and she looked up at Maya with concern.

"Maya, what happened to your arm?" Carly asked softly.

Maya's smile faltered. She pulled her sleeve down quickly, feeling the flush of embarrassment. "Oh, it's nothing. No big deal."

Carly's expression didn't waver, and she reached out, gently touching Maya's arm. "You sure? It looks like more than nothing."

Maya winced slightly at Carly's touch but forced herself to meet her friend's gaze. "It's just... Cole and I had a.... tense conversation. It got a little physical, but it's fine. Really."

Carly frowned, her concern deepening. "A 'tense' conversation? Maya, that really sounds like something. And it certainly doesn't *look* fine."

Maya sighed, her gaze dropping to the floor. "It's... complicated. I thought I could handle it, but it got out of hand. I'll be okay."

Carly looked like she wanted to say more but stopped herself. They settled into their seats as the professor started class, Carly's concern still evident in the way she glanced over at Maya from time to time.

"Please promise me you won't meet him alone again." Carly whispered as their lecture started. "Take one of us with you to be nearby. Just in case."

Maya glanced over at her friend, seeing sincerity and concern in her eyes, and nodded. "That's probably a good idea."

THE REST OF THE DAY passed in a blur of lectures and assignments. Maya's thoughts often drifted back to the conversation with Carly and the pain still echoing from her encounter with Cole. As she walked across campus to her next class, she tried to clear her mind, but her thoughts remained restless.

As she stepped out of her final class, the campus buzzed around her. The warm afternoon sun bathed the quad in golden light, a stark contrast to the turmoil swirling inside her. Maya's feet carried her toward the coffee shop almost automatically, thinking a caffeine boost might help her focus for the evening ahead. But as she walked, something—or rather someone—caught her eye.

A familiar figure stood by the bench near the library, his head bent slightly as he chatted with a few classmates. Her heart lurched in recognition. It was Ryan.

Maya slowed her pace, her eyes narrowing in on his face, and that's when she noticed the bruises. The purplish-blue swell under his left eye, the dried cut on his lip. It looked like he had been in a fight. A serious one.

Her pulse quickened, a mixture of panic and concern bubbling up inside her. Without even realizing it, she quickened her pace, weaving through the students scattered across the quad. The closer she got, the clearer his injuries became, and her heart practically stopped.

"Ryan!" she called out worriedly.

Ryan's head snapped up at the sound of his name. He blinked, clearly surprised to see her rushing toward him. "Maya?" he said, his tone caught between casual and confused. "Hey, what's—"

But Maya was already in front of him, her eyes scanning his face with disbelief. "What happened to you?" she gasped, her breath trembling as her gaze lingered on the bruises. "Are you okay?"

Ryan hesitated, shifting his weight uncomfortably. He glanced around, nodding a farewell to the people he had been speaking to as the sun dipped lower in the sky. He extended his arm in front of him, gesturing for her to walk with him, a question in the movement.

"It's nothing," he tried, offering a weak smile that only emphasized the cut on his lip. "Just... a rough night."

"A rough night?" Maya repeated incredulously, falling into a slow pace next to him. She felt her hands clenching into fists as her chest tightened. "Ryan, you look like you were in a fight. Who did this to you?"

Ryan's shoulders dropped slightly, the tension in him visible now as he let out a small sigh. "It's not a big deal, Maya. Really."

"Ryan," she pressed, stepping closer and stopping their progress, her words soft but firm. "Don't lie to me. This isn't nothing."

He winced, running a hand through his hair as if trying to gather his thoughts. She suddenly knew with certainty what he would say before he finally lowly admitted, "It was Cole."

Maya's heart sank, a sick feeling spreading through her chest at this confirmation. "Cole? He did this?" The idea of Cole—someone she had once loved, someone she thought she knew—hurting Ryan made her nauseous

Ryan glanced away, his jaw tightening before he nodded. "Yeah. He was... upset about everything. You, mostly. It got a little heated, and..." He gestured vaguely at his bruised face, his tone almost nonchalant, as if he didn't want to make a big deal of it.

Maya felt a wave of guilt crash over her. This was her fault. She had caused this, even if unintentionally. "I'm so sorry," she whispered, thick with emotion. "I didn't mean for any of this to happen."

Ryan turned back to her, his eyes softening. "Hey, stop. This isn't your fault. Cole... he's dealing with a lot right now, but what he did is on him, not you."

"But I feel like I dragged you into this," Maya murmured, her throat tightening. She felt tears prickling at the corners of her eyes. "I shouldn't have let it get this far."

Ryan reached out, his hand gently brushing her arm in a gesture meant to comfort. The intimacy of his touch sent a small, electric tingle through her skin, the same sensation she'd felt in the coffee shop. "Maya, I was already in this," he said softly, his voice steady. "Cole was gonna come after me one way or another."

She looked up at him, her eyes searching his face. The bruises, the split lip—they were all because of her. Yet here he was, trying to reassure her, to make her feel better. It was overwhelming, and she wasn't sure what to say.

"I hate that you got hurt because of me," she whispered, barely audible. Ryan had always been there for her, never judging her for her choices or criticizing her dreams.

Ryan's smile was small, but genuine. "I'd do it again if it meant making sure you were okay."

The tenderness in his tone made her heart ache, and before she could think twice, Maya stepped forward and wrapped her arms around him in a tight hug. She pressed her face into his shoulder, breathing in the faint scent of his cologne. It felt safe here, in his arms, and she allowed herself to stay there for just a moment longer than she should have.

Ryan tensed for a moment before his arms came around her, holding her, and she felt his body relax into the embrace. He didn't say anything, but the calmness of his presence was enough to quiet some of the chaos in her mind.

Finally, after what felt like both an eternity and no time at all, Maya pulled back, her cheeks flushed with emotion. She looked up at him, her eyes glimmering with gratitude. "Thank you," she whispered thickly. "For everything."

Ryan cleared his throat, his own emotions barely masked behind his usual calm demeanor. "Anytime," he replied softly.

Maya hesitated, not wanting to let the moment end. "Can I walk you home?" she asked, feeling tentative.

Ryan shook his head gently, giving her a reassuring look. "I'll take you home, Maya. Let's get out of here. Are your classes done for the day?"

She wanted to protest, but the look in his eyes told her not to. She nodded quietly, and they walked side by side toward his car. Ryan kept close to her, not saying much, but the comfort of his presence was all Maya needed at that moment.

They made it to the car before she noticed how tenderly he was walking, as if his torso was causing him pain, too.

Maya settled into the passenger seat, buckling her seatbelt as Ryan started the car. The soft hum of the engine filled the silence between them, as she struggled with guilt over his injuries. Ryan shifted the car into gear and her gaze drifted to his hands on the steering wheel.

It wasn't until then that she noticed the bruises—dark, angry marks across his knuckles, stark against his skin. Her heart skipped a beat. He had fought back.

The realization hit her all at once, like a wave that crashed too late. Of course, he had. Why hadn't it occurred to her until now? When Cole had grabbed her, all her focus had been on her own safety, on Cole's frightening grip and the suffocating tension that had followed. She hadn't thought about Ryan having a different reaction and responding to that aggression with some of his own.

"Ryan..." she spoke with a mix of concern and guilt. Her eyes lingered on his hand, fingers tightly gripping the wheel as if he could hide the damage.

He glanced at her, then followed her gaze down to his knuckles. He flexed his fingers, the bruises more macabre in the shifting light of the dashboard.

"It's nothing," he muttered, brushing it off with a casual shrug. But Maya knew better.

"How... bad did it get?" She hated asking, but now the question felt too big to leave unspoken.

Ryan exhaled slowly, eyes fixed on the road. "Bad enough," he finally admitted. "We... did some damage to each other. It wasn't pretty."

Maya swallowed, guilt churning through her. "Because of me," she whispered.

"No." Ryan shook his head sharply. "Not because of you. Because Cole couldn't let go, and I couldn't stand to see you hurt. That's not on you, Maya." His tone softened, his knuckles whitening as he tightened his grip. "I told you already that I'd do it again if I had to. Your reasons for breaking up were valid then and are still valid now, and I feel like garbage for even encouraging you to meet him for coffee in the first place."

Her chest tightened at his words, and she turned her gaze back to the window, watching the world blur by. She tried not to let her guilt suffocate her. "You didn't know." She murmured, but Ryan didn't seem to hear her.

Chapter 11

Ryan's POV

Ryan's hands stayed steady on the steering wheel, but his mind churned as they drove in silence. The bruises on his knuckles throbbed slightly, but that pain was easier to ignore than the tension gnawing at him. He kept stealing glances at Maya—her quiet concern, the way she had gone from anxious to protective in the span of seconds.

Out of the corner of his eye, he saw her shift in her seat. "Ryan," she began, hesitantly. "You and Cole... you live together, right?"

Her concern hit him harder than he expected, a pang of discomfort twisting in his gut. Of course, she'd think about that. The thought that he was still going home to the same apartment as the guy who'd hurt her.

Ryan nodded, keeping his voice even. "Yeah, we do."

Maya bit her lip, clearly wrestling with something. He tried to ignore the way that unconscious action made his entire body vibrate and want to free her lip for her. "How... are you going to handle that?"

He let out a slow breath, realizing he hadn't fully thought it through yet. "I don't know. I'll figure it out. I'm not going back tonight, though." He cast her a quick glance, trying to sound casual. "I crashed at Carly's place last night. Just needed space. Grabbed some stuff this morning after Cole left for class."

Her brow furrowed as she turned toward him, the concern in her eyes palpable. "Yeah, you should stay somewhere else for a while. Until things calm down."

Ryan's heart made an uncomfortable flip. The way she said it, the way she cared—it stirred something deeper in him, something that made his chest tighten. He wasn't used to this, wasn't used to her worrying about him. That had always been Cole's place as the object of her affections.

"I'll figure it out," he repeated, softer this time. "Don't worry about me."

But she was still staring at him, her eyes filled with that same quiet worry. And when they finally stopped at a red light, Ryan felt her hand gently brush his arm. He froze, the warmth of her touch sending a jolt through him—tingles, sharp and electric, spreading from where her fingers rested.

"Ryan... I do worry about you," she whispered, her words almost a confession. Her hand lingered a second too long before she pulled it back.

The light turned green, and Ryan forced himself to focus on driving. But he couldn't stop thinking about it—the way her hand had felt on his arm, the way her words clung to him. He didn't know what to do with that. With her concern. With how it made him feel something more than just protective. He was angry, yes, but there was something else, too. A kind of quiet, unspoken longing bubbling up.

After a few more moments of silence, he pulled up outside her building. He shifted into park but didn't move, just sat there, the current between them thick and heavy.

"Why don't you crash on our couch tonight?" Maya suggested, quiet but firm. "I mean, it's probably better than going back after... well, everything."

Ryan turned to her, surprised. "I don't want to impose. You and Shelby—"

Maya cut him off with a soft smile. "You wouldn't be imposing. Besides, it's just for a night or two, right? We've got a couch and extra blankets. It's better than being out there or going back to Cole. It's the least I can do."

Ryan let out a breath, clearly torn. The last thing he wanted was to drag more people into this, but the exhaustion in his eyes was hard to miss.

After a pause, he finally nodded. "If you're sure."

"I'm sure," she said, her tone leaving no room for argument.

Ryan gave a small, grateful smile. "Thanks, Maya. Really."

Maya leaned back in her seat, feeling the tension between her shoulders ease just slightly. "Anytime."

Without thinking, she reached over and placed her hand gently on his arm again. "You don't have to deal with this alone."

The touch was brief but sent tingles up his arm. Ryan glanced at her, and for a split second, he could almost imagine what it would be like to lean in for a kiss.

Clearing his throat, Ryan pulled away from the moment. "I'll grab a few things from my car. Be right in."

Maya nodded, stumbling slightly as she got out of the car. She offered him one last look before heading inside. As the door clicked behind her, he couldn't help but wonder how long they could tiptoe around the tension that now seemed to spark between them.

He shook his head, laughing at himself. Her concern for him didn't mean that she saw him as anything other than a friend that she had had for years. He would be a fool to think her feelings towards him were more than platonic.

Ryan sighed and headed to the trunk of his car, slinging a duffle bag over his shoulder as he made his way toward Maya and Shelby's apartment. He hesitated briefly before walking up the steps. Staying here, with Maya and Shelby, felt... complicated, but it was better than going back to Cole.

He approached the door and heard a soft conversation inside. He paused for a moment before knocking, hearing Shelby's voice over the faint clinking of pans.

"I just don't get it. What's going on with him and Cole? I've never seen either of them like this." Shelby's words carried from the kitchen, a mixture of curiosity and concern lacing them.

Maya's response was quieter, though still clear. "It's complicated. I told you that Cole and I met for coffee and things escalated." She paused, the weight of the memory making her voice falter. "When Cole lashed out at me, I called Ryan in a panic and he picked me up. That seems to have pissed Cole off even more and that catapulted into their own issues."

Shelby clattered something onto the stovetop, sighing. "Issues like punching Cole?"

"I don't think I have that full story, but something like that."

"God," Shelby muttered softer now. "I'm glad Ryan was there and all, but what now? They're still roommates."

Maya sighed, and Ryan could hear the strain in her reply. "I don't know. I offered him the couch tonight. I couldn't let him go back there."

Ryan took that as his cue, knocking louder than necessary before opening the door the rest of the way and stepping inside. Both girls looked up as he entered.

"Hey," Maya said, a smile tugging at her lips. She was kneeling by the couch, spreading out blankets and fluffing a pillow. "I've got your bed all set."

"And dinner's almost ready too," Shelby added with a grin from the kitchen, where she was stirring something in a pan. "So, you're in luck."

Ryan chuckled lightly, his hand rubbing the back of his neck as he closed the door behind him. "You guys are doing too much. I feel like I should be helping."

Maya stood, brushing her hands together. "Nonsense. You're the guest."

Ryan set his duffle down by the couch, glancing between the two of them. "Thanks. Really. You didn't have to do all this."

Shelby waved him off with a spoon. "Please, Ryan, after everything, we're just glad you're not out there dealing with Cole."

Maya nodded, though her eyes were on him, studying his face, lingering a little too long on his bruised lip and the darkening area beneath his eye. "Shelby's right. You're not imposing."

Ryan shrugged slightly, forcing a small smile. "Well, thanks for letting me crash here. I really appreciate it."

Shelby leaned against the counter, watching the two of them with a knowing smile. "We're all in this together. Besides, it's kind of nice having a guest so we don't end up eating these leftovers for days. Stay as long as you need."

Ryan glanced at Maya, their eyes meeting briefly before she smiled again. "Yeah," she said softly. "We're here for you."

That tension from earlier—the one that seemed to sit just under the surface between them—was still there. The room felt warmer, more comfortable than he expected, and yet there was still that tug, a pull that made him question if it might be worth confessing his developing feelings for Maya.

Before he could say more, Shelby turned off the stove with a flourish. "Dinner's ready!" she called. "Come on, you can at least help set the table, honored guest."

Ryan laughed, grateful for the lightness Shelby brought to the room. He moved toward the kitchen, glad for a distraction, just as he realized how hungry he really was.

As they sat down for dinner, the conversation drifted into easier topics, but every now and then, Ryan found his eyes flicking toward Maya, who seemed lost in her own thoughts. He found himself relaxing more than he had in days, laughing and talking as Shelby kept everything upbeat and lively.

After dinner, he had helped the girls clean up the best dinner he had had since Maya and Cole had broken up and he has lost the deliciousness of the girls' cooking. Then, he ended up on the couch that Maya had made up for him, trying his best to turn off his brain.

He was in the middle of a restless night on the couch when he heard the creak of a door. Blinking awake, he saw Maya stepping into the living room, wearing an oversized shirt that fell just above her knees. It was clearly a shirt she'd borrowed, adding a casual, almost endearing quality to her appearance.

"Hey," she whispered, seeing he was awake. "I'm just getting some water. How are you feeling? Do you need any painkillers or anything?"

Ryan rubbed his eyes and sat up, feeling a twinge of discomfort from his bruises. "I'm okay. Just a bit sore. Thanks for asking."

Maya gave him a concerned look as she filled a glass from the kitchen sink. "You shouldn't have to be on the couch. It's not comfortable... if you want, you can take my bed. I'll just crash here on the couch."

Ryan hesitated, his pride and discomfort warring within him. "I don't want to put you out. I'll be fine."

Maya shook her head, setting her glass down and walking over to him. "I insist. You're already dealing with enough and you need to get some sleep. Just let me help."

She sat down on the couch next to him, her presence comforting and warm. Ryan felt more hesitant. Sleeping in her bed felt like it would be overstepping boundaries.

"Are you sure?" he asked, though the earnestness in her eyes made it clear she was.

"Definitely," she said, offering a small smile. "And if you're uncomfortable, I'll be right here."

Ryan nodded, still reluctant. "I appreciate it, but I'm really okay on the couch."

Maya thought for a moment and then offered a compromise. "You know what? My bed's pretty big. We can both sleep there. It'll be more comfortable, and we'll have plenty of space. As long as you're okay with it."

Ryan's heart about stopped as the words left her mouth and the weight of her offer sunk in. Sleep in her bed? *With* her? The thought sent his mind spinning. He felt like accepting this offer would put them both in a scenario that they weren't ready for yet, but a more selfish part of him just wanted to sleep.

He glanced at her. She was waiting for his response, completely sincere in her offer, unaware of the effect it was having on him. The oversized shirt she wore, slightly disheveled, hung loosely off her frame, and he found himself wondering what it would be like to lie next to her, feel her presence next to him in such an intimate space.

"Are you sure you're okay with this?" Ryan asked unsteadily. He wasn't just asking for her sake. He needed reassurance for himself, too—needed to know that he could handle this without crossing those boundaries, without letting his own feelings complicate things.

Maya nodded, her smile gentle but firm. "Absolutely. It's just sleep, Ryan. You've had a rough few nights. You deserve some actual rest."

Her words were simple, but they offered a sense of calm he didn't expect. He couldn't deny the exhaustion in his body, the dull ache in his muscles, and the way his mind kept drifting to worst case scenarios. He wasn't in the mood for more discomfort—not tonight.

Taking a breath, he nodded slowly. "Okay... if you're sure."

Maya stood up and gestured to the bedroom door. "I'm sure. It'll be fine."

As he followed her into her room, Ryan's body still buzzed with a low hum of tension. Lying in the same bed as her felt sensual in a way he hadn't fully prepared for. His pulse quickened slightly as he sat on the edge of the bed, watching as Maya casually pulled the covers back and slipped in, giving him plenty of space.

"See? Plenty of room," she reassured, patting the space beside her.

Ryan chuckled nervously, slipping under the covers on the opposite side. The mattress dipped slightly with his weight, and for a moment, he was hyper-aware of every inch between them. The soft rustle of sheets, the warmth of the bed—it was all so tempting in a way that he was sure she hadn't intended.

He kept his hands to himself, staring at the ceiling for a moment as Maya shifted beside him. The scent of her shampoo lingered in the air, and he tried not to think too much about the fact that they were both lying here, together, in the middle of the night. His mind wandered briefly to what it would be like to reach over, to close the space between them, but he shoved that thought away as quickly as it appeared.

Get a grip, he told himself. This isn't about that.

But despite the nervous energy, there was comfort, too. Maya was here. They were okay. And for the first time since everything with Cole had exploded, Ryan felt a sense of peace wash over him.

As his body relaxed into the bed, exhaustion began to pull at him. The tension in his muscles slowly unwound, and he let himself focus on the steady rhythm of Maya's breathing beside him. The events of the day started to fade, replaced by the quiet calm of the room, and before he knew it, he was drifting off to sleep.

Maya's POV

Maya stirred slowly, blinking as the soft morning light filtered through the curtains. It took her a moment to orient herself, to remember that she wasn't in bed alone. Ryan's arm was draped loosely over her waist, his chest pressed up against her back, and his steady breath brushed the back of her neck.

For a second, she lay perfectly still, uncertain of how to move without waking him. The steady rise and fall of his chest behind her was comforting, his weight grounding. There was something undeniably intimate about the way they'd settled during the night, tangled together despite the space the bed allowed.

Then, the sudden awareness of his body—the heat, the proximity—struck her all at once. And the firm pressure against her lower back sent her spiraling into full consciousness.

Oh. *Oh.*

Her cheeks flamed instantly. Oh God. She swallowed, her mind racing as she registered what she was feeling. The unmistakable sign of his body's reaction in sleep, pressing into her. Her pulse quickened, her thoughts spinning between awkward embarrassment and something else—something deeper, more instinctual, that simmered beneath the surface.

Maya's heart thudded in her chest, conflicted by the rush of sensations. She had known Ryan for years, trusted him immensely, but she'd never imagined waking up like this. It shouldn't feel so... natural.

She had been with guys, of course, and was no stranger to this particular sensation, but it had been intentional in the past. This felt more like she was violating Ryan by being aware of his body's reaction, though.

She closed her eyes, willing herself to stay calm, but instead, her senses sharpened—every breath he took against her, the way his arm tightened around her waist in his sleep, like his body was instinctively pulling her closer. Her skin tingled, heat radiating where they touched, and she suddenly felt acutely aware of her own desire—a soft ache deep in her core, a pull she wasn't sure she wanted to acknowledge.

She shouldn't be feeling this. Not when he wasn't even awake and not when she had already complicated his life with problems.

But her body didn't seem to agree. She squeezed her eyes closed as tight as she could and took a few deep breaths to stop herself from thinking about how it would feel to roll over and throw her leg over his hip, positioning him in just the right spot.

Carefully, she tried to shift, attempting to slide out from under his arm without disturbing him. Her breath was shallow, her hands shaking just slightly as she moved. But just as she thought she'd managed to slip free, his grip tightened, drawing her back against him.

Maya froze, her heart slamming in her chest. Her pulse roared in her ears, and she was hyperaware of everything—his breath on her neck, his hand splayed possessively across her torso, and the solid presence of him pressed against her back.

A low, guttural groan escaped his throat as he shifted. That sound only served to send another wave of desire burning through her heated body.

Her mind screamed at her to stay calm, to think rationally, but her body was betraying her. She could feel the desire building inside her, a knot of need twisting in her core. It had been so long since she had felt this—since anyone had touched her like this, even unintentionally. She shouldn't want this. She wasn't *supposed* to want this.

"Maya?" His voice was low, gravelly with sleep, breaking the silence.

Her breath hitched. "Yeah?" she whispered, unable to keep her voice steady.

"Sorry," Ryan muttered, his arm starting to pull away from her waist. But before he could fully retreat, Maya felt him freeze, realization seeming to dawn in the way his whole body went rigid behind her.

For a long moment, neither of them said anything, the silence thick with tension. She could practically feel his thoughts racing, trying to piece together what had just happened.

"Ryan," she whispered. "It's okay."

He finally moved, loosening his hold on her, but the space he left behind was almost worse—cold and hollow, where just moments ago he had been. Maya took a breath, trying to collect herself, but the confusing mix of relief, loss, and desire churned in her chest.

Ryan shifted away, clearly trying to give her space, but she could feel the tension between them like a physical thing. "I didn't mean to—"

"It's fine," she interrupted quickly, maybe a little too bright and a little too forced. "It's... it happens."

Right. That was what she told herself, hoping it would ease the awkwardness. Hoping it would make the yearning in her chest quiet down. But it didn't. Instead, it amplified everything—the unsaid words between them, the unspoken attraction that had always simmered beneath the surface, growing more intense now that they were both unattached and completely over their former relationships.

She sat up, pulling the blanket around her as if it could shield her from the storm of emotions swirling inside. What was wrong with her? This was *Ryan.* The same Ryan that lived with her ex-boyfriend. The same Ryan that had all but disappeared from her life after her breakup until just a few weeks ago.

Ryan was sitting up now too, running a hand through his hair, his jaw tight. She could tell he was trying not to make this a bigger deal than it needed to be, but his avoidance, his hesitation, only made her more aware of what had passed between them. The unspoken tension crackled in the air like static, humming in her veins.

She hadn't paid much attention the night before to his lack of a shirt, as she had seen him shirtless enough times during the time she dated Cole. Now, though, her eyes involuntarily traced the line of his jaw down his chest and abdomen to where the blanket bunched up on his lap, where his—

NOPE. She wasn't going there.

She didn't know what to say, how to bridge the gap between them. Part of her wanted to brush it off, to make some joke to ease the tension, but another part of her—the part that hadn't been touched in so long, that ached for connection—wanted to tell him to stay. To pull him close again.

But she couldn't. She wouldn't.

Instead, she forced herself to smile, though it felt tight. "I'll make coffee," she said quickly, slipping out of bed before he could respond. The oversized shirt she wore clung to her as she moved, the fabric brushing against her skin in a way that did nothing to relieve her overly sensitive skin.

As she walked toward the kitchen, she took several deep breaths, body still humming from the unexpected contact. Her head told her it was just a normal physical reaction, while another part of her desperately didn't want it to be just that.

In that moment, it didn't even occur to her to feel guilty about what this might do to Ryan's relationship with Cole.

She quickly busied herself making coffee and getting things ready for breakfast. The sound of the shower running signaled Ryan was up, though Maya couldn't allow herself to think too much about that without clenching her legs together. Soon Shelby joined her, padding quietly into the kitchen.

"Coffee?" Maya offered, holding up a fresh mug.

"Yes, please." Shelby accepted, leaning against the counter with a grateful sigh. "You're a lifesaver."

Maya smiled, pouring the coffee. "So, anything on the agenda for today?"

Shelby took a sip and nodded. "Eh, I have rounds in a few and then I'm going to try and wrap up a few things for my residency applications."

Maya raised an eyebrow. "Still finding time for casual hangouts with your 'no-labels' person?"

Shelby smirked. "It's not that serious. We're just keeping it light. I don't want to get too involved while I'm applying for residencies and don't know where I'll end up in a few months."

"I hear you," Maya said, cracking a few eggs into a bowl. "Still, you've been seeing each other for a while now."

Before Shelby could respond, the bathroom door creaked open, and Ryan appeared, hair still damp, wearing a fresh T-shirt and jeans. He glanced around and grinned. "Good morning. Am I missing out on juicy gossip?"

Shelby chuckled, crossing her arms. "Nothing you don't already know. Just chatting about life as a single lady and whatnot."

Ryan pulled out a chair and sat at the table, eyeing Shelby with a teasing glint. "Ah, so your infamous label-free gentleman. Still playing it cool, huh?"

Shelby shot him a look. "Don't start."

"I'm just saying," Ryan added, grabbing the coffee pot to pour himself a mug. "You seem pretty invested in keeping things light for someone who mentions it every time we talk."

Maya couldn't help but laugh. "He's got a point."

"Whatever." Shelby rolled her eyes good-naturedly, her smile betraying her amusement. "I'm keeping my options open, okay? What about you two? Any exciting updates for life after this?"

Ryan leaned back, his expression softening as he looked over at Maya. "Still figuring that part out, I guess."

Maya watched Shelby react to this look out of the corner of her eye, but thankfully she didn't press them. Instead, she grinned and shook her head. "Well, whatever happens, you both better not lose touch after graduation."

Maya smiled through her jolt of anxiety. There was so much more to figure out between now and then but falling out of touch with her friends was not in her plans.

Chapter 12

Ryan's POV

Ryan leaned back in his chair, cradling the mug of coffee in his hands and watching the steam rise. The warmth felt good, but his mind was elsewhere—Shelby's talk of the future had him itching to check his email, but he left his phone in his pocket. His empty inbox could wait a little while longer.

Shelby pulled him out of his thoughts. "I don't think I'm ready for all the adulting that comes after school. Residency applications are one thing but the residency itself and then getting an actual position... where am I supposed to find time to do normal adult things or even see anyone?"

Ryan chuckled softly, trying to refocus. "You've got more going on than you let on. I have a sneaking suspicion that you're a master at juggling everything, though."

Shelby shrugged. "I guess there's only one way to find out!"

He glanced over at Maya, who was staring into her coffee, lost in her own head. He hesitated before he continued, shifting the topic. "Speaking of future adulting... you're still shooting for New York, right?"

Maya blinked, as if waking from her thoughts. "Yeah. I have another meeting with my advisor to kinda finalize things today. It's mostly about if there are any other tweaks needed to my portfolio." She looked down, uncertainty bleeding through her words.

Ryan could see the weight she carried. He didn't want to push her, but part of him wanted to say more, to offer something more substantial. He ultimately decided to keep it simple. "You've got this."

Shelby leaned over, nudging Maya. "You're gonna crush it, Maya. Seriously."

Ryan nodded, watching Maya's small smile appear. It wasn't much, but he could tell she appreciated the support. Still, something in her eyes remained distant, guarded, like there was more she wasn't saying. He hated that he couldn't just fix everything for her.

They quickly ate before Shelby went to gather her things, Ryan stood and stretched. His body still ached from the altercation with Cole, but it wasn't the bruises or the sore muscles that weighed on him—it was the tension that had wrapped itself around everything since then. "I better head back and see how things are at the apartment. Hopefully, Cole's cooled off in the last few days."

The casual way he said it felt forced, even to his own ears. He rubbed the back of his neck, trying to ease the discomfort that crept in at the thought of facing Cole again. Maya, as always, noticed. Her tone was soft, a thread of worry woven into her words. "Are you sure that's a good idea? I don't want things to get worse."

Her concern hit him deeper than he expected. She always cared, always looked out for others, but this was different. He could see it in her eyes—she wasn't just worried about the fight. She was concerned about him and that hadn't changed despite his less than stellar start to their morning. "I'll be fine, Maya. I need to talk to him, get it over with. If it gets bad, I'll leave again. Don't worry."

Her hesitation was obvious, her lips parting as if she wanted to protest. But she held back. "Okay," she finally said, her eyes lingering on his. "But if you need anything..."

"I'll text you," he promised, offering her a reassuring smile that felt more natural than the earlier forced bravado. "Promise."

Shelby came back into the room, tossing a playful jab about not causing trouble, and Ryan laughed, grateful for the break in tension. But as they gathered their things and left the apartment, his mind was already racing ahead, to the confrontation that waited for him at home.

In the car, Ryan's thoughts were heavier. Every mile closer to his apartment felt like a step towards inevitable conflict. He could still see Cole's rage, feel the moment things had snapped between them. Maybe today would be different. Maybe it wouldn't. Either way, it had to be addressed.

He pulled into the parking lot, his fingers drumming against the steering wheel in a nervous rhythm. For a moment, he just sat there, staring at the building, wondering how this was going to go down. He wasn't ready for this friendship to end, but then again, he wasn't sure he ever would be.

Before getting out, Ryan grabbed his phone and shot Maya a quick text: *About to go talk to him. Don't worry—I'll be fine. I'll let you know how it goes.*

With that, he slid the phone into his pocket, took a deep breath, and headed inside, bracing for whatever came next.

Ryan unlocked the door, stepping inside the apartment as quietly as possible. His senses were on high alert, and he scanned the space for any sign of Cole. The apartment was eerily silent, save for the faint hum of the fridge in the kitchen. Ryan felt his pulse quicken as he moved further inside.

He hadn't seen Cole since their altercation two days before, and as much as he wanted to hope for a calm conversation, he knew that was likely a lost cause at this point.

Ryan's phone buzzed in his pocket. It was a text from Maya: *"Good luck. Text me if you need anything."*

He stared at the message for a second longer than necessary, a small smile tugging at his lips.

From down the hallway, the door to Cole's room creaked open. Ryan tensed, shoving his phone back into his pocket as he heard footsteps approaching.

Cole appeared in the doorway, his face bruised and still carrying the remnants of anger. His eyes locked on Ryan, and for a moment, the volatility in the room felt suffocating. Neither of them spoke, the silence stretching thin between them.

Finally, Ryan broke the ice. "We need to talk."

Cole folded his arms, leaning against the doorframe. "Yeah, we do."

Cole's hostility was clear as day, and Ryan felt the familiar anger rising in his chest. He swallowed it down, determined not to let this escalate like before. "I didn't come here to fight. I just want to figure this out."

Cole scoffed, shaking his head. "Figure what out, Ryan? The fact that you've been sneaking around with Maya this whole time?"

Ryan's jaw clenched. "That never happened, and you know it."

"Oh, do I?" Cole's volume rose, his frustration boiling over. "You expect me to believe that after everything I've finally seen these past few weeks, that there was *nothing* between you two? You've been acting like some knight in shining armor, always coming to her rescue—don't think I haven't noticed. I've opened my eyes to the shit I had always let slide between the two of you."

Ryan's hands tightened into fists at his sides. He could feel the frustration bubbling up again, but he forced himself to stay calm. "I've been trying to help her because she's my friend, and she needed it. That's all."

"*Friend.*" Cole spat the word out like it was poison. "Is that what you call it? Cause from where I'm standing, it looks a hell of a lot more like you've been waiting for your shot since the day we broke up. That's what happens, right? You all just pretend things are fine and spring this shit up out of the blue."

Ryan stepped forward, his look steady but filled with quiet intensity. "You're angry, and I get it. But blaming me for what happened between you and Maya isn't going to fix anything. You broke up—she's allowed to move on. And so are you. I don't know how to prove to you that nothing happened."

Cole's eyes narrowed, and for a split second, Ryan thought they might actually get through this without another fight. But then, Cole's face twisted in a mix of hurt and betrayal. "Move on? You want me to move on while you just slide in and take my place?"

Ryan exhaled sharply, his patience wearing thin as Cole ignored his last statement. "No one tried to take your place, Cole. But you've got to stop holding onto this idea that Maya's still yours. She made her decision."

That did it.

Cole lunged forward, his fist connecting with Ryan's already bruised jaw. Pain exploded across Ryan's face, but he barely had time to register it before he swung back, his fist slamming into Cole's cheek with a solid *thud.*

The fight was brief but brutal. Fists flew, knuckles connected with skin, and the next thing Ryan knew, he was on the ground, blood dripping from his split lip. Cole wasn't much better off, cradling a black eye and wincing from the impact.

Ryan immediately regretted coming back to the apartment. He regretted fighting back beyond defending himself. He regretted letting things get this bad with Cole without ever noticing it, too wrapped up in his own things.

For a few seconds, neither of them moved, both catching their breath in the aftermath of the fight.

"I'm done," Ryan muttered, wiping the blood from his mouth. "I can't prove nothing happened, and you won't listen to anything other than your own version of events. This gets us nowhere and I'm not doing this anymore."

Cole didn't respond, just glared at him from across the room. Ryan slowly stood up, his body aching from the blows they'd exchanged.

Without another word, Ryan turned and walked out of the apartment, the door slamming shut behind him.

He'd given it a shot—tried to talk it out—but now there was no turning back. Whatever was left between him and Cole, it was broken beyond repair.

Ryan stared at the door for a long moment before finally turning away, his fists clenched, knuckles throbbing from where they'd connected with Cole's jaw. Another fight. Another round of angry words and accusations.

He ran a hand through his hair, trying to shake off the frustration that gnawed at him, but it clung to him like a bad hangover. This wasn't how things were supposed to be.

He stepped into his car and sat there for a moment, his heart still racing. He needed to go somewhere, anywhere that wasn't his apartment. Somewhere he could breathe.

Mark's place.

He grabbed his phone, thumb hovering over the text to Maya, but he paused, guilt gnawing at his insides. Cole's words replayed in his head, sharp and venomous: *"from where I'm standing, it looks a hell of a lot more like you've been waiting for your shot since the day we broke up."*

Ryan shook his head, gripping the steering wheel tighter. He hadn't been waiting for Maya... right?

He sighed and sent a quick message to Mark instead:

"Hey, can I crash at yours for now? Things blew up again."

Mark's reply came almost instantly: *"Yeah, of course. We've got the spare room ready. Come over whenever."*

Ryan pulled away from the curb, his thoughts tumbling over themselves. He hadn't had a girlfriend in over a year—so what? It wasn't like he had been hung up on Maya. But now? Now it might be a different story.

Admitting that to Cole right now wasn't the best idea, though, and regardless of something developing with Maya, he now knew his friendship with Cole likely wouldn't last. The thought should have been devastating after years of friendship, but Ryan just felt resigned to it now.

The drive to Mark's felt like a blur, and when he finally parked outside their apartment, the weight in his chest had only grown heavier. He grabbed his bag from the backseat, the one he'd tossed most of his stuff in after the first blow-up with Cole, and headed inside.

Mark opened the door before he could knock, giving him a once-over before stepping aside. "You okay, man? You look rough."

Ryan forced a smile. "Yeah, just tired."

Mark's girlfriend, Emily, poked her head out from the kitchen, her face softening in sympathy. "You can stay as long as you need, Ryan. We're happy to have you."

"Thanks," Ryan muttered, feeling more exhausted than ever. He was grateful for their hospitality, but the tension inside him wasn't easing.

Mark gestured toward the hallway. "Come on, I'll show you the spare room."

Ryan followed him, dropping his bag on the floor when they reached the small, neatly made bed. He sank onto the mattress with a sigh, running a hand over his face.

Mark leaned against the doorframe, crossing his arms. "Want to talk about it?"

Ryan shook his head. "Not much to say. Things with Cole... they're a mess. We tried talking again, and it just blew up."

Mark nodded, his brow furrowing. "Sorry, man. That sucks. You think there's any way to fix it?"

"I don't know," Ryan admitted, feeling a knot of tension forming in his shoulders. "He's convinced there's been something going on between me and Maya since well before they broke up, and no matter what I say, he doesn't believe me."

Mark's eyebrows rose slightly, but he didn't comment right away. "I guess you can't really prove the absence of something happening," he finally said. "Is there something going on now, though?"

"No," Ryan said immediately, but the word felt heavy in his mouth. "I mean... I care about her, but nothing has ever happened. Nothing that he's accusing me of, anyway." He paused, chewing the inside of his cheek as he remembered this morning again. "I don't think she would want it to, regardless."

Mark gave him a long look, as if weighing his words. "Look, you and Maya pursuing something now is fine if that's what you two want, but you should consider that you probably won't be able to do so and remain friends with Cole simultaneously. These accusations of his are just confirmation that he's not okay with even the idea of you and Maya. I can't imagine how he'd react to that being a reality."

Ryan stood up, restless, needing to move. "I don't know, man. I just want things to go back to not being so damn complicated."

Mark sighed and clapped him on the shoulder. "Don't I know it, man. Take your time. You need to sort yourself out before you can approach him or her to untangle this mess."

Ryan nodded, though his mind felt more jumbled than ever. As Mark left him alone, Ryan stared at the wall. He needed to be honest with himself that he was starting to fall for Maya. Maybe he just needed to accept that his falling out with Cole was permanent. Sighing, he got out his laptop, intent on catching up on some work he had been procrastinating for the past few days.

Chapter 13

Maya's POV

Maya and Carly walked across the campus, enjoying the crisp air of the early spring. Carly was talking animatedly about her recent projects, her excitement palpable, but Maya's thoughts kept drifting back to Ryan and the ongoing tension with Cole.

Maya nodded absently, trying to refocus her mind on Carly's words. She caught sight of Cole in the distance, standing near a bench with a few friends. Her heart skipped a beat. Cole's face was still marred by the remnants of the fight—a black eye that was almost impossible to ignore. He looked worn, and the visible bruises and swelling made it clear he'd had a rough time.

Maya felt as though there was ice in her veins suddenly. She'd been dreading the possibility of running into him, especially knowing how he'd reacted the last time they spoke. Even from a distance, his presence was enough to put her on edge.

Carly noticed Maya's shift in demeanor. "Hey, are you okay? You look like you've seen a ghost."

Maya's gaze remained fixed on Cole. "Yeah, it's just... Cole. I didn't expect to see him today."

Carly followed her line of sight and frowned. "Oh, wow. That sucks for him. I guess he's still feeling the aftermath of the fight."

Maya nodded, her nerves jangling. "Yeah. I haven't seen him since everything went down but seeing him like this... geez."

Carly reached out, squeezing Maya's arm gently. "You don't have to talk to him if you don't want to. I mean, you've been through enough already."

Maya forced a tight smile, her eyes flickering back to Cole. "I know. I just didn't expect to feel this unsettled seeing him again. It's hard to shake the feeling that things could go south quickly if he's not in a good place mentally."

As Cole turned and caught Maya's eye, his expression shifted from a pained grimace to something that resembled resignation. He didn't approach them, but Maya could feel the weight of his stare. It was as if he was still carrying the emotional weight of their past interactions.

Carly noticed the change in Maya's expression. "Do you want to avoid him, or do you want to address it? We can head the other way if you prefer."

Maya took a deep breath; her heart caught in her throat. "I think... I'd rather just keep my distance for now. I'm not sure what to say, and I don't want to make things worse."

Carly nodded in understanding, guiding Maya away from Cole. "Got it. Let's go grab some coffee or something. He doesn't deserve your attention, anyway."

As they walked away, Maya couldn't shake the lingering anxiety. She knew she had to focus on her upcoming meeting with Whitman, but the sight of Cole and the tension of their past interactions were hard to let go of.

Maya attempted to redirect the conversation back to Carly's projects, feeling like a terrible friend for having her mind be all over the place lately.

They walked towards their favorite campus café, Carly keeping up a steady stream of conversation about her design project, her enthusiasm a welcome distraction.

When the girls stepped inside into the warm air, Carly went to place their order while Maya found a table. The rich aroma of coffee and pastries filled the air, providing a soothing backdrop. Maya took a deep breath, trying to push aside the knot of fear that had formed after her last encounter with Cole.

Carly joined her a few minutes later, carrying their drinks. “Here you go,” she said, setting a steaming cup of coffee in front of Maya. “I went for the usual—caramel latte for you and a black coffee for me. I figured you could use a pick-me-up.”

Maya smiled gratefully, taking a sip of the warm beverage. The sweetness provided a small measure of comfort. “Thanks, Carly. You’re seriously the best.”

Carly took a sip of her coffee and glanced at Maya with a concerned expression. “You sure you’re okay? I know running into Cole wasn’t easy, but you don’t have to put on a brave face with me.”

Maya shrugged. “I’m just trying to process everything. Seeing him like that... I don’t know. It brings up a lot of emotions. I’m worried about him, but I also feel afraid of him and who he’s become. I never knew him to be violent before.”

Carly nodded, her expression sympathetic. “That makes sense. It’s tough to balance empathy with self-preservation. Just remember, you don’t owe him anything. You’re allowed to prioritize your own well-being.”

Maya gave a small, appreciative nod. “Yeah, I’m trying to remind myself of that. We’ve all got a lot on our plates right now, with graduation coming up and everything. I need to stay focused on my future.”

Carly leaned in, her tone shifting to something lighter. “Speaking of your future, have you gotten any bites or job options opening in New York?”

Maya brightened at the change of topic. “Yeah, I’m excited but also a little nervous. I think I’m pretty much done with my portfolio, and I’m hoping to get some solid feedback today to have some nibbles coming in soon.”

Carly grinned. “You’re going to crush it, Maya. I have no doubt. And once you’ve got that all sorted, maybe you can finally relax.”

Maya laughed softly. "I hope so. I could use a break. But first, I need to get through today's meeting and make sure everything's on track."

Maya glanced at her phone. She hadn't heard from Ryan since this morning, and it had been hours without a peep. Seeing Cole, she suddenly realized that the conversation earlier today might have gone the same way as their last one, which was alarming.

Carly noticed and gave Maya a curious look. "Everything okay?"

Maya nodded, her fingers hovering over the screen as she contemplated messaging him before shoving her phone back into her pocket.

"Just thought I heard it go off. I'm hearing things now, I guess."

Carly laughed. "Don't worry, we'll all still love you when you go crazy."

Maya smiled back, her mood lifting. "I might already be halfway there, but that's good to know."

As they finished their coffee and went on with their day, Maya decided that she was done with the constant drama with Cole and she was only going to focus on herself and her future now. She was mentally exhausted by constantly worrying and wondering about him. It was time to distance herself from whatever he had going on now.

Ryan POV

Ryan stood outside the apartment complex, his breath coming out in uneven bursts as he tried to calm himself. His knuckles were still sore, his body tense. This couldn't keep happening.

He rubbed a hand across his face, feeling the lingering sting where Cole had landed a punch. He had only stopped back now that he knew Cole was at work and shouldn't be here so he could grab more things since he didn't know when things would be better between the two of them now.

He hated imposing on Mark and Emily and knew how much they valued their alone time and space. Yet here he was, selfishly doing so anyway.

Sighing, he went in and gathered what he could, loading things haphazardly into his trunk and backseat.

Within an hour, Ryan was done and headed back to Mark and Emily's place.

Once he brought in his essentials, Ryan sat on the edge of the bed, staring down at his hands. They were still trembling slightly, adrenaline not yet fully worn off from the fight even though it had now been a few hours. He clenched them into fists, trying to push the images of the morning out of his mind.

Cole's words about being the reason everything fell apart rang in his ears. Ryan had tried to keep calm, but the anger was still there, simmering beneath the surface. And Cole had known exactly how to push his buttons.

Ryan's throat tightened at the thought. The more Cole threw the accusations at him, the more he started to question their friendship and what it had even been based on. A few shared classes and random housing assignments freshman year?

He rubbed his hands over his face, trying to shake the thoughts away. He needed to focus on something else, something productive. Classwork. He had plenty of that to keep him busy, and it was better than sitting here, stewing in his own thoughts.

Opening his laptop, he pulled up the group project he was working on with Krista and Emily. But as he stared at the screen, his mind wandered back to last night at Maya and Shelby's place. He hadn't wanted to impose, and he *definitely* hadn't meant to end up in bed with Maya. But when she had offered, looking at him with those soft eyes, it had been impossible to refuse.

The feeling of her body pressing up against him was hard to forget. He hadn't even meant to touch her, not consciously. His body had apparently acted of its own accord in the night, pulling her close and the fact that she fit so perfectly against him hadn't helped.

For a fleeting moment this morning, he hadn't cared about anything else—only her. How warm she was. How right it had felt, even though it was probably wrong. Before he had noticed his body's reaction to her in the morning light.

He closed the laptop with a snap, realizing there was no way he could concentrate on school right now.

The guilt and affection oscillated in him. He wasn't supposed to feel like this about Maya. She was Cole's ex, and he was supposed to be Cole's friend. He couldn't help but feel like that bridge had burned, though, and regardless of that he couldn't help his developing feelings for Maya. He wasn't sure he even wanted to. Running a hand through his hair again, Ryan sighed.

He was supposed to be here, focusing on his future, on school, on moving forward. But instead, all he could think about was how it had felt being that close to Maya, her body against his, the way she had curled into him during the night, trusting him without hesitation.

The door creaked open, snapping him back to the present. Emily peeked her head in, her smile soft and understanding. "Hey, you all settled in?"

Ryan nodded. "Yeah, just trying to get some work done."

Emily stepped inside, keeping the door open behind her. "How are you holding up?"

He shrugged. "Could be worse."

She sat down on the edge of the bed, glancing at him. "Mark told me about what happened. You don't have to talk about it, but just... if you need to, I'm here. We both are."

Ryan sighed, grateful for her support. "Thanks, Em. I just need some time to figure all this out. Cole... he's a mess right now, and I don't know how to fix it."

Emily reached over, giving his arm a squeeze. "You don't have to fix it. Just take care of yourself. Cole is responsible for sorting his own stuff out."

Ryan nodded, though her words didn't fully take the weight off his shoulders. He wasn't sure what the next few days would bring, but for now, at least, he had space. Space to think. To breathe. To figure out what the hell he was going to do next.

Chapter 14

Emily's POV

Ryan still looked lost in thought when Emily's spoke up, breaking through the haze. "Hey, you look like hell. Let me clean you up."

He blinked, meeting her concerned gaze. "It's fine, I've had worse."

"Uh-huh," she replied, unconvinced. "You don't have to be tough all the time, you know."

Ryan sighed but didn't argue. "Fine," he muttered, getting to his feet. "Let's get it over with."

Emily stood and led him out into the small kitchen. She grabbed the first aid kit from one of the cabinets, motioning for Ryan to sit at the kitchen table. The light overhead flickered slightly, casting shadows across the room, but it was warm and brightened up the place.

As she watched Ryan slump into the chair, the exhaustion seemed to be weighing him down like a boulder. The bruise forming on his cheek and the cuts on his knuckles were clear signs that he had taken as many hits as he had given in this latest fight. She knew Ryan—he wasn't the type to throw punches without being pushed. But ever since everything blew up with Cole, he hadn't been able to catch a break.

Mark lingered in the doorway; his brow furrowed in concern as he watched Ryan sit down. He crossed his arms, casting a look at Emily that said, *Is he okay?*

She sighed softly, pursing her lips and grabbing the first aid kit from the cabinet before getting out some supplies. Then she began carefully dabbing a cotton ball on Ryan's split eyebrow. The cut wasn't deep, but it would probably leave a mark. She caught the slight flinch in his jaw and muttered, "Sorry," though she barely applied pressure. Mark walked into the room, leaning against the counter nearby with his arms folded, watching them in silence.

"You're sure you're good? I think this might need stitches." Emily pointed out, eyeing the cut critically. "I really should have offered this earlier, huh?"

Ryan shook his head. "Nah, I'll be fine."

She bit back a sigh, typical Ryan, brushing off the damage like it was nothing. As she continued cleaning his face, her thoughts drifted back to everything that had gone down between Cole and Maya.

Looking at Ryan now, Emily couldn't help but think about how he'd always been there for Maya. It wasn't just as Cole's friend but as Maya's, too. In a way that had been much steadier and accepting than anything she'd seen between Cole and Maya in those final months.

The truth was, she'd never really thought Cole and Maya fit. Not the way they should have on paper, at least. Especially not towards the end, when everything about them felt strained. Cole had these expectations, this rigid view of their future, and it seemed like Maya had been shrinking away under the weight of it all. In contrast, Ryan had never tried to control her or shape her into anything she wasn't. He had just... cared. Quietly, but always there.

Ryan had always been friendly and welcoming to all his friend's girlfriends, but he had been closer to Maya than any of the rest. Emily had never perceived it as being disrespectful or crossing any boundaries, though.

She glanced up at him now, catching the way he stared past her, lost in thought. His face was tense, not just from the fight but from something deeper.

"You don't have to talk to him again anytime soon," Emily said softly, breaking the silence. "Not if you're not ready."

Ryan exhaled, rubbing the back of his neck. "I know. But I don't know what to do about our place..." He trailed off. "It's wild that after all these years we've known each other, he really thinks I would have betrayed him like that. We didn't have an affair. It was never even a thought."

Emily paused, the cotton ball still in her hand. The way Ryan spoke, the past tense, as if whatever he'd felt for Maya was buried in some distant chapter. And yet, there was something unspoken—a hesitation, a flicker—that hinted things weren't necessarily the same anymore.

"Ryan..." she started but trailed off, deciding against voicing that thought, so Mark spoke up.

"Okay, you didn't like her *then*." Mark asked, raising an eyebrow. "But now?"

Ryan shrugged, avoiding their eyes. "It's not like that," he muttered, clearly uncomfortable. "Cole's just... wrong. I just care about her wellbeing. He *hurt* her. Physically. I couldn't stand that. I'd do the same if you hurt Emily. I'd defend her, too, and tell you that you needed to back the hell up and leave her alone." He suddenly looked directly into Mark's eyes.

Emily froze for a moment, surprised by the intensity in Ryan's voice. The kitchen, which had been filled with quiet clatter suddenly felt still. Ryan's words hung heavily in the air.

Mark straightened up, his eyes meeting Ryan's with a mix of surprise and respect. "I get it, man. I wouldn't expect any less." He was calm, but there was gravity to his response, like he understood the seriousness of what Ryan had just said. He glanced briefly at Emily before looking back at Ryan. "None of us would stand by something like that."

Ryan exhaled slowly, his shoulders relaxing slightly, but the tension wasn't completely gone. The weight of his words settled around them.

Emily, watching the silent exchange between the two men, noticed the subtle shift in Ryan's expression. It was more than frustration or anger—it was protectiveness, but also something else. Something softer. She'd seen that look before but maybe hadn't really understood it until now.

"You've always had her back," Emily said quietly. "Even when things weren't complicated."

Ryan's jaw clenched slightly, but he didn't deny it. Instead, he just nodded, glancing down at the table. "Yeah," he said softly. "But things *are* complicated now."

Mark leaned forward, resting his arms on the table. "So, what are you going to do about it? You can't stay in limbo forever. You're living here, and you're not talking to Cole. But Maya? You still care about her. And maybe you need to have that conversation with her."

Ryan's gaze flickered up, meeting Mark's. "I don't know. I wasn't trying to be the guy who—"

"The guy who what?" Emily interjected gently. "The guy who actually treats her with respect?"

Ryan ran a hand through his hair, sighing. "I don't want to hurt anyone, especially not Maya. And the last thing I need is for her to think I'm just swooping in after everything with Cole. That was never the plan."

Emily's heart softened as she listened to him wrestle with his thoughts. He wasn't the kind of guy to make a move just because he had the opportunity. He genuinely cared about Maya, but it was clear to Emily—and probably to Mark, too—that this was more than just a sense of duty.

Mark spoke up again, his tone softer now. "Ryan, you're not Cole. You're not forcing her into anything. If something happens between you two, it'll be because it's what's right for both of you."

Ryan's eyes darkened slightly as he leaned back in his chair. "That's the problem," he muttered. "I don't know if it's right. Not with all this mess."

Emily stepped closer. "You care about her, Ryan. That's not the problem. The problem is Cole, and the way he treated her. Maya's going to need people who are there for her, people she can trust. You're one of those people."

Ryan looked up at Emily, and for the first time since the fight, there was a vulnerability in his eyes. "What if I'm part of the problem?" he asked quietly, almost like he was afraid to voice the thought out loud. "What if I lose her altogether because she doesn't feel the same?"

Mark shook his head firmly. "You've never treated Maya the way Cole has. And you sure as hell didn't hurt her. You'll never know how she feels, though, without talking to her."

Emily nodded in agreement, gently but firmly stating. "You're not part of the problem, Ryan. You're part of the solution."

For a moment, Ryan didn't say anything, just stared down at his hands. Then, finally, he nodded, though his expression remained conflicted. "Maybe."

Mark gave him a reassuring pat on the shoulder before standing up. "Look, man, you've got time. But just know, whatever happens, you've also got people who have your back."

Ryan managed a small smile.

Emily exchanged a quick glance with Mark before deciding to drop it, at least for now. But the thought stuck with her—something had shifted.

Emily turned back to the task at hand, finishing up with the cut. "There," she said, satisfied. "You're patched up."

Ryan sighed, grateful for the distraction. "Thanks."

Mark cleared his throat. "Well, now that you're not bleeding all over the place, how about we focus on something a little more productive?"

Ryan jumped on the opportunity. "Yeah, the project," he said, relieved. "Let's get to work."

They gathered around the kitchen table, spreading out their notes and diving into the work. Mark wasn't in their finance classes, but he had his own work to get caught up on. Ryan threw himself into it, seeming thankful for the distraction, but as they worked, Emily kept catching little glimpses of him—his focus intense, but every now and then, his expression would soften. As if, despite his best efforts, his mind kept wandering back to something—or someone—else.

Emily smiled to herself, knowing exactly where his thoughts were drifting. She just wondered when Ryan would finally do something about it.

Chapter 15

Maya's POV

As Maya and Carly walked across campus, the midday sun cast long shadows between the buildings. It was a perfect day for walking—crisp air, just warm enough to enjoy but cool enough to keep from sweating.

Carly had her hands shoved into the pockets of her jacket, her pace relaxed as she fell into step beside Maya. "I've got my meeting with Professor Chang later today. I'm hoping to get some feedback about some Portland positions," she said, glancing at Maya. "What about you? You feel ready?"

Maya laughed softly. "We're going over my portfolio—" she paused, pushing her hair behind her ear, "—and I've been looking at this firm in New York called Hayes & Martin. They specialize in digital strategy for startups, and I think I'd be a good fit." She shrugged, trying to downplay her nerves. "I'm submitting an application for an entry level position there."

Carly raised her eyebrows, clearly impressed. "Hayes & Martin? Wow, that's huge! I mean, seems competitive as hell, but if anyone's got the talent to land that, it's you."

Maya gave a small smile, her anxiety still gnawing at her. "Thanks, I hope so. I just feel like everything is riding on this, you know? New York's where I see myself after graduation, and this application could make or break that becoming reality."

Carly nudged her playfully. "You're overthinking it. You've got the skills and the experience. Besides, you've worked too hard to not get something big."

Maya nodded, letting out a heavy sigh. "Thanks."

Carly changed the subject. "So, are you thinking long-term with Hayes & Martin, or is this just for the foot in the door?"

"If I can get the position, I'm hoping it'll be a long-term position, and I can really gain a network out there. New York is where I want to be, so... it'd be ideal." She contemplated aloud. "But I guess time will tell if it would open other doors while I'm there."

They continued their walk, Maya's thoughts bouncing between her career aspirations and the lingering tension from everything that had happened. She hated this anticipation of not knowing how things were going to go. She was a big fan of spoilers and hated living out the tension in real time.

The two arrived at the advising office building, the sight of it pulling Maya back to the present.

At least for now she had this step forward to focus on. New York. Hayes & Martin. If she could get through this meeting and land this position, everything else would work out. It had to.

Maya sat nervously tapping her fingers against the armrest of the chair. Professor Whitman sat across from her, reviewing the papers in front of her. Her office was always warm, filled with books, academic papers, and the framed photo of New York's skyline that had initially caught Maya's eye. It had felt like a sign, like her future was somehow tied to that place.

"Alright, Maya," Professor Whitman said, adjusting her glasses as she looked up. "I've been going over your portfolio updates, and I have to say, it's looking really solid. You've clearly put a lot of effort into refining your style, and it shows."

Maya felt a flicker of relief, though her anxiety still hummed beneath the surface. "Thank you. I've been trying to focus on projects that would showcase my skills for places like Hayes & Martin. I'm submitting my application there soon."

Professor Whitman smiled knowingly. "Ah, Hayes & Martin. You've got a good eye for opportunity. They're a top-tier firm and I think you'd be a great fit there."

Maya's heart picked up its pace. "That's what I'm hoping. New York feels like the right place for me. I just need to get my foot in the door."

Whitman leaned back in her chair, thoughtful for a moment before nodding. "Well, as it turns out, I might have something else that could interest you." She rifled through a few papers on her desk before pulling out a business card. "There's another firm I think you should consider—Wexler & Greene. They're not as large as Hayes & Martin, but they're well-respected in the industry, particularly for creative branding and digital strategy."

Maya blinked in surprise. "Wexler & Greene? I think I read something about them."

"I thought you might have," she said with a smile. "I had a friend recently reach out who works there—Sara Morgan, head of the digital strategy team. I mentioned you to her after our last meeting, and she's very interested in seeing your work. She thinks you'd be a strong candidate for a position, especially with your background."

Maya's eyes widened, and she leaned forward slightly in her chair. "You recommended me?"

"I did," Professor Whitman said, smiling at her reaction. "Your portfolio speaks for itself. I'd suggest reaching out to her directly, sending her your portfolio and resume. Let her know you're interested in applying, and I'm confident you'll at least get an interview."

The idea of another potential opportunity in New York made Maya's head spin. It felt almost too good to be true. "I—I didn't expect this. I'm so grateful, Professor. I'll definitely reach out to her."

"I thought you'd be interested," she said, her expression kind. "I know you've had your eye on New York for a while now, and this could be another door opening for you. Don't put all your eggs in one basket, Maya. It's always good to have options."

Maya nodded, absorbing this advice. "Yeah, you're right. Thank you so much for the recommendation. I'll apply to both, and hopefully one of them works out."

Whitman stood up, extending her hand to Maya as she rose from her seat. "You're going to do great things, Maya. New York will be lucky to have you."

She shook Whitman's hand, feeling a sense of gratitude mixed with renewed determination. "I really appreciate your support. I won't let you down."

After a few more words of encouragement, Maya left the office, the weight of the meeting lifting off her shoulders. She felt lighter, more hopeful. Two solid options in New York? It seemed like the pieces of her future were finally starting to come together.

Maya stepped out of the office, still processing everything. She spotted Carly waiting outside the café, tapping on her phone, looking up just in time to see Maya heading over.

"Hey!" Carly greeted her, tucking her phone away. "How did it go?"

Maya let out a breath, her smile widening. "Really well. Better than I expected, actually. She thinks I should apply to another firm in New York. It's through a friend of Whitman's and so I got her business card and a recommendation to apply there, too!"

Carly's eyes lit up as she looped her arm through Maya's. "Oh my god! That's huge, Maya! New York's practically calling your name at this point."

Maya chuckled. "Yeah, it feels like it's getting real now. I'm kind of freaking out."

"As you should!" Carly laughed, steering her toward the café. "But seriously, you've been prepping forever. You've got this."

"I hope so," Maya murmured. "I haven't even sent the applications yet. I've been so focused on tweaking my portfolio. But, hearing that recommendation was... kind of a game changer. Now I've got two major opportunities to apply for."

Carly grinned, nudging her playfully. "So basically, you're about to be the next big thing in New York. I'm so proud of you!"

They reached the café and grabbed a table outside. After they ordered, Carly leaned back in her chair, sipping her iced coffee. "So, when are you sending your stuff off? Like, this week?"

Maya made a face. "I want to, but you know me. I'll probably go over my resume and portfolio a thousand more times before hitting 'send.'"

"Classic Maya," Carly teased with a grin. "But seriously, don't overthink it. You've got everything lined up. I mean, both seem like great firms. Just imagine that on your resume."

"I know," Maya admitted, the excitement bubbling in her chest again. "It's just... New York. It's been such a long road to get here yet it somehow also feels like it's all happening so fast."

"Ugh, I get that! But, hey, you're ready for this. And when you're in New York, you'll be living the dream," Carly said, then paused, her expression shifting. "I'll be all the way over in Portland."

Maya met her gaze, feeling a bittersweet pang. "Yeah, that's true. We're going to be so far apart. But I think it's amazing you're going to Portland. It feels like the right place for you."

Carly's grin returned. "Yeah, I think so. Portland's been on my radar for a while now. The freelance scene there is great, and the agencies are super creative. Plus, you know... Rachel's there."

Maya raised an eyebrow. "Ah, so it *is* about Rachel."

Carly laughed, but there was a flicker of something more serious in her eyes. "Maybe a little. But I'm not doing anything solely for her. It's just... Portland feels like the place I need to be right now. Even if Rachel wasn't there, I think I'd still want to go. And Chang thinks that I'm ready, so there's that."

Maya nodded, feeling a mixture of pride and sadness. "Yeah... It's just weird to think about how close we are now, and soon we'll be on opposite sides of the country. Portland and New York are basically worlds apart. But I am so glad that you are going to be doing what you love to do in a place you want to be, too."

Carly sighed, swirling her iced coffee. "Yeah, it's gonna suck being that far. But we'll make it work. We've been through too much to let some distance mess with our friendship."

"Agreed," Maya said with a small smile. "We'll visit each other. Fly across the country when we can. Keep each other updated on our crazy post-grad lives."

Carly raised her cup. "Here's to Portland and New York. We're going to crush it in our own way."

Maya clinked her glass against Carly's, feeling a renewed sense of excitement. "To Portland and New York. We've got this."

Maya sat at the small desk in her room, eyes scanning her portfolio once again. Her resume was open on the screen, and the blinking cursor seemed to mock her, daring her to make just one more change. It wasn't that she didn't trust her work, but with so much riding on these applications, it was hard to shake the feeling that there was something—*anything*—that could make it better.

She didn't even notice Shelby leaning against the doorframe until she cut through the silence. "You're going to drive yourself crazy if you keep staring at that thing, Maya."

Maya exhaled, leaning back in her chair. "I know, but I just... I don't want to screw this up. If something's off—"

"Nothing's off," Shelby interrupted, walking over and peering at the screen. "It's perfect. You're perfect for these firms, and I'm not just saying that because I'm your friend." She shot her a teasing grin, but her tone softened. "You've put in so much work. There's nothing left to tweak. Just hit send already."

Maya rubbed her temples. "I just don't want to miss anything. What if Sara Morgan doesn't even look at it? Or what if they both just think I'm not a fit?"

"That won't happen." Shelby perched on the edge of Maya's bed, crossing her legs. "Look, I get it. But you've been talking about moving to New York for how long? This is your chance. They'll see how amazing you are, and you'll crush it. I just know it."

Maya sighed and glanced at her laptop again, the email draft to Sara Morgan already open. She'd spent so much time crafting it, yet her fingers hesitated over the send button.

Shelby nudged her with her foot. "Do it. You know you want to."

With one more deep breath, Maya attached her finalized resume and clicked the button. The email disappeared from her screen, and a sense of finality washed over her. A few more clicks and she sent one to Hayes & Martin as well. "Done."

"Finally," Shelby teased, leaning back on her hands. "Now, take a break. You've been obsessing over this for days."

Maya turned to face her, the tension in her shoulders finally easing. "What about you? How are things going with your classes?"

Shelby groaned, throwing her head back dramatically. "Don't even get me started. I have this massive paper due for one of my classes, plus all the residency stuff. I feel like I'm drowning half the time."

"Sounds intense," Maya replied sympathetically. "How are you managing it all?"

"Barely," Shelby laughed, though it didn't quite mask her exhaustion. "I keep telling myself it'll all be worth it in the end. It's just... a lot right now, you know? The whole 'adulting' thing isn't as glamorous as we thought."

Maya smiled. "No kidding. But you've got this. Just like you said to me, you've worked hard for this moment. You're almost there."

Shelby raised an eyebrow. "That's my line. You can't just throw it back at me."

"If the shoe fits," Maya teased.

"Fine, fine. You win this one." Shelby stretched, her arms high above her head. "But seriously, it'll all work out for both of us. Now that you've finally sent those emails, we should celebrate or something."

Maya chuckled, feeling lighter than she had in days. "Maybe after I get a response."

"Deal."

Chapter 16

Ryan's POV

Ryan sat on the edge of the couch, controller loosely in hand, barely paying attention to the game unfolding on the screen. Mark and Brandon were deep in conversation, shouting instructions about the midfield, but Ryan's mind was a mess. It had been weeks since the last fight with Cole, but the tension still weighed on him, and even the usual escape of game night couldn't drown out his thoughts.

Cole's absence from these nights was noticeable. At first, it had been a relief, the tension between them unbearable, but now it just felt strange. Ryan knew Cole was still angry, and honestly, he wasn't ready to face him either. Avoidance seemed easier, so they had moved things to Mark and Emily's place for now.

"Ryan, you alright?" Mark cut through his thoughts.

Ryan blinked, realizing he had missed yet another pass. "Yeah, sorry," he muttered, forcing himself to focus on the game for a second. "Just distracted."

"Distracted?" Brandon glanced over at him with a smirk and an eyeroll. "What's going on this time?"

Ryan shrugged, unwilling to dig into the mess of thoughts swirling inside. Every time he closed his eyes, he could still feel Maya's body pressed against his, the touch of her skin, the softness of her breath. That night in her bed had left him reeling, and he'd been avoiding her ever since, too.

"Is it Cole?" Alex asked, glancing back at him. "He's still pissed, huh?"

Ryan nodded. "Yeah. We haven't talked since the fight. And I've kinda been avoiding him, too. Easier that way."

"And Maya?" Emily asked from the small dining table, where she was typing away at her laptop. She didn't look up, but Ryan could feel the weight of her question hanging in the air.

Ryan's insides twisted at the mention of Maya. "Same there," he admitted quietly.

Mark exchanged a glance with Emily before looking back at Ryan. "Oh, come on. You and Maya have been friends for years. I thought you were going to talk to her ages ago."

Ryan shifted uncomfortably, eyes fixed on the floor. "Yeah, but now I just feel like I've made a mess of things. And at this point, I've been avoiding her for so long she probably wants nothing to do with me, either. I don't know how to move forward."

The words tasted wrong, and he hated how they felt in his mouth.

Mark raised an eyebrow, sensing something in Ryan's hesitation. "Do you want to? Move forward with her?"

Ryan clenched his jaw, trying to shove the thoughts away. "Maybe. Maya's always been great. She's focusing on her own stuff now, though, and I need to do the same. She doesn't need to be dragged into more shit because Cole *would* start some if we ever were to get together."

Emily finally looked up, a confused expression on her face. "So, you're avoiding both of them and hoping that'll fix things?"

Ryan exhaled sharply. "I don't know. It's not just them. I've been applying for jobs, too: New York, LA, Chicago, Hartford. Anything risk management, really."

"New York?" Brandon glanced over, surprised. "That's where Maya's headed, isn't it?"

Ryan tensed, not sure if he was ready to acknowledge what that might mean. "Yeah. But I'm keeping my options open," he said quickly, trying to steer the conversation away from the train of thought his mind wanted to take of Maya and him together in New York.

Emily spoke up again. "Ryan, you can't avoid this forever. Either of them."

Mark nodded in agreement. "And you've got to figure out what you want. Not what Cole wants, or even Maya, but *you*."

Ryan leaned back, rubbing a hand over his face, feeling the weight of it all. What did he want? He'd been running on autopilot for weeks now, avoiding his feelings, avoiding confrontation. But deep down, he knew that wouldn't last forever.

Mark nudged his shoulder gently. "You've gotta be honest with yourself, man. If you do end up with a position in New York especially, this isn't going to go away. And those Wall Street positions are opportunities you don't want to pass up if and *when* they come your way."

Ryan gave a slight nod. "I know. I don't want to get my hopes up that I could have that kind of future and then end up in different parts of the country, though,"

He picked up his controller, forcing himself to focus on the game, though every time he closed his eyes, Maya's presence still lingered, the memory of her body against his impossible to shake.

Carly POV

Carly leaned back in the booth, a grin tugging at her lips as she took in the lively atmosphere of the bar. Everyone was buzzing with energy. It felt like a collective exhale after weeks of stress, applications, and sleepless nights.

Emily was the first to raise her glass. "To the future," she declared, her eyes bright with excitement. "Wherever that may be."

Carly smiled, feeling the weight of her own relief. "I'll drink to that." She clinked her glass against Emily's, then glanced around the table. "I still can't believe it's happening. Interviews. Actual interviews." She leaned into Ryan, who was seated next to her. "Where are you most excited about?"

Ryan swirled his drink, clearly deep in thought. "New York would be amazing, and I have my family in Hartford, but I'm not ruling out Chicago or LA either. Gotta keep my options open."

Carly nudged him with her elbow. "You always did like to have a backup plan."

Ryan gave her a wry smile but didn't say anything more. His eyes flicked briefly toward Maya, who was laughing with Mark and Emily across the table. Carly noticed the glance, the brief tension in his jaw. She could tell that there was more brewing under the surface but tonight wasn't about dissecting the drama.

Maya, for her part, seemed lighter tonight. Carly couldn't blame her. Landing an interview in New York was huge, and she was already dreaming about what it could mean. Plus, the Chicago one was solid backup. Maya had worked hard, and it was finally paying off. She practically radiated excitement, even if there was a flicker of something else every time she glanced around.

Mark leaned forward, practically bouncing with energy. "Chicago better get ready for me and Emily," he said with a grin. "We've both got interviews there."

"Different firms, though," Emily added, nudging him. "You're gonna be stuck in that stuffy architecture office while I'm trading stocks in a high-rise."

Mark rolled his eyes. "Hey, someone's gotta *design* those high-rises."

Maya grinned, chiming in, "If I end up in Chicago, we'll have to keep the group alive. Even if Carly ditches us for Portland."

Carly shrugged playfully. "Hey, don't knock it till you try it. I've got two interviews lined up, and if things go well, it's all but a done deal. Besides, freelance life in Portland seems like a dream."

Emily raised her glass again, laughing. "Portland, Chicago, New York—it doesn't matter where we end up. We'll make it work."

The group clinked glasses again, toasting to their futures. Carly glanced around, feeling the excitement crackling between them all. They were on the cusp of something big, and for the first time in a while, she wasn't thinking about all the stress and uncertainty. Just the possibilities.

Chapter 17

Maya's POV

As the night wore on, Maya excused herself from the table, her head buzzing pleasantly from the drinks. The bathroom was tucked toward the back of the bar, and as she splashed some water on her face, she couldn't help but smile at her reflection. It felt surreal—the interviews, the opportunities in front of her. It was all happening.

She dried her hands, feeling a new rush of excitement as she headed back out. The music was louder now, and the energy in the bar had shifted into the late-night vibe.

As she rounded the corner, she nearly collided with someone. Her hands shot out instinctively, and she found herself face-to-face with Ryan.

"Whoa, sorry—" she started, but the words caught in her throat as their eyes met.

Ryan looked a little startled himself, but then he smiled, the tension in his shoulders easing. "Maya. Hey."

Maya took a small step back, feeling the moment settling between them. "Hey. Getting another round?"

Ryan nodded, his expression unreadable for a second. "Yeah. Needed a breather from all the chaos over there."

She chuckled, glancing back toward the table where the rest of their friends were still caught up in conversation. "It's definitely lively tonight."

He hesitated, and for a moment Maya thought he might walk away. But instead, he stepped closer, leaning against the bar beside her. "How are you feeling about everything? The interviews, I mean."

Maya tried to suppress that rush of excitement she felt again. "I'm nervous, but mostly excited. New York would be a dream, of course. And Chicago... well, I'm keeping that in my back pocket."

Ryan nodded, but there was something in his eyes, something thoughtful, almost... distant. "You'll do great. They'd be lucky to have you."

"Thanks." Maya smiled at him. "What about you? You've got some pretty big interviews coming up, too."

Ryan shifted, his hand wrapping around the glass in front of him. "Yeah, I applied to a few finance companies in New York, too. LA, Chicago, Hartford... I'm keeping my options open."

"New York, huh?" Maya's heart skipped a beat. "That'd be something, wouldn't it?"

Ryan met her eyes, and for a moment, the noise of the bar seemed to fade away. "Yeah, it would."

They stood there for a beat too long, the air between them thick with unspoken words. Maya couldn't quite put her finger on it, but there was something in Ryan's gaze tonight—something different. She felt her pulse quicken, her skin still warm from their brief collision.

Ryan cleared his throat, breaking the tension. "I should, uh, get those drinks."

Maya nodded, stepping aside to let him pass. "Right. I'll see you back at the table."

As Ryan moved to the bar, Maya watched him for a moment longer before getting another drink of her own and heading back to their friends.

The night had been a blur of laughter, excitement, and drinks. They had all been buzzing with the news of their first-round interviews, and the celebration had lasted longer than anyone expected. Carly and Andrew were at one end of the booth, talking animatedly with Brandon and Shelby, while Emily and Mark were leaning into each other, sharing an inside joke.

As the bartender called the last round, Carly stretched, tapping on her phone. "Okay, folks. No one's driving, right? We'll split up in rideshares." She shot a teasing glance toward Maya and Ryan. "And don't worry, I'll make sure we don't cram you all together."

Maya rolled her eyes but couldn't help the flush creeping up her neck. She felt Ryan's presence beside her—he was sitting just close enough that their arms brushed occasionally, sending little sparks of awareness through her. Her excitement from the night, mixed with the alcohol, made her more aware of it than usual.

As Carly sorted out the ride details, Maya looked around the group. "I'm with...?" she asked, pretending to check her phone as if it mattered.

"You're with Ryan," Carly said, casting a glance between the two of them. "Andrew, Brandon, and Shelby are in the first car. Mark, Emily, and I in the second. You two are in the last one." Carly grinned mischievously. "Don't have too much fun without us."

Ryan raised an eyebrow but didn't say anything, slipping into his jacket as they all started to gather their things. Maya's heart gave a quick thud in her chest as she caught his eye. She couldn't ignore the way her body reacted to him—especially with a few drinks loosening her up.

They stepped out into the cool night air, laughing at nothing in particular, their happiness blending with the city sounds around them. Maya felt tipsy but in a good way, that warm buzz settling in as they waited for their car.

Shelby, Brandon, and Andrew piled into the first ride-share, waving as it pulled away. Carly, Mark, and Emily climbed into the next, exchanging more playful teasing about Ryan and Maya being left behind together.

Maya suspected exactly what she was doing, because these rides didn't make sense since she and Shelby were going to the same place, and she had heard that Ryan was staying with Mark and Emily. Ryan had been distant, though, so she didn't mind the slight meddling if it gave her a chance to talk to him. He couldn't avoid her in the back of a car together.

Still, she stood close to Ryan on the sidewalk, feeling the chill of the night creeping into her bones. "Looks like it's just us," she said, trying to keep her tone casual.

"Yeah," Ryan agreed, glancing at her briefly. His face was unreadable, but there was something in his eyes that made her reluctant to look away.

Their ride pulled up, and they slid into the backseat, sitting close, side by side. The car was quiet compared to the lively bar, and the space between them felt charged in the silence.

Maya could feel every brush of his arm against hers, the strength of his body radiating through his jacket. As the city lights flashed by outside, she realized how much her heart was pounding. She glanced sideways at Ryan, noticing how his jaw clenched and relaxed, as if he was thinking about something.

She felt bold. Maybe it was the alcohol, maybe it was the way his presence made her feel electric, but she wasn't in the mood to hold back.

"So... it's all so exciting, isn't it?" she said softly, leaning slightly into him. The feel of his arm against hers sent a thrill through her.

Ryan hesitated before answering quietly. "Yeah. I hate the uncertainty of it all, though." His gaze flicked toward her, his eyes dark in the dim light of the car.

Maya felt her pulse quicken. There was tension between them that she couldn't ignore anymore. "Well," she murmured, trying to reassemble her brain enough to form a coherent sentence. "I guess we'll both be looking for a new city to call home soon."

He nodded, but there was something unsaid lingering in the air between them. Something that felt heavy and inevitable.

Her heart thudded in her chest, and before she could overthink it, she shifted closer, letting her shoulder rest fully against his. When he didn't move away, didn't flinch, she took a breath and looked up at him. "Ryan..."

He turned toward her, his expression unreadable. "Yeah?"

Without thinking, Maya leaned in. Her lips brushed his, tentative at first, testing the waters. She half-expected him to pull away, to stop her before things went too far. But instead, he responded. The second his lips pressed back against hers, a spark ignited.

The kiss deepened quickly, and the tension that had been simmering between them for weeks—months—boiled over. Ryan's hand slipped to her waist, pulling her closer, and Maya melted into him, her heart racing. The chemistry between them was undeniable, the weight of everything unsaid finally surfacing.

When they finally broke apart, breathless, Maya pulled back just slightly, their foreheads resting together. The car still hummed along the quiet street, but inside it, the world had shifted. She didn't know what this kiss meant or what it would mean for them moving forward but she couldn't bring herself to regret it. Not even for a second.

She leaned in and kissed him again, a deep-seated desire igniting in her core as she tried to position herself better against him and have as much of their bodies touching as possible. Ryan's grip on her hip and neck tightened and she could feel his body was ready for her, too.

This time, when they broke apart, it was due to the vehicle stopping in front of her apartment building. Ryan's eyes stayed closed for a moment longer, but when he finally opened them, there was a carnal need reflected in his gaze. "Maya, I..."

Maya kept her eyes locked on him, trying to convey precisely how much she needed this moment. "Come upstairs?" she asked breathlessly.

Ryan cleared his throat, releasing his hold on her slowly. "Maya..." he said, his voice thick, clearly torn. He ran a hand through his hair, leaning back. "I don't think that's a good idea, Maya," he said, though there was hesitation in his words.

Maya's heart sank a little, but she nodded, understanding. "Yeah... I get it."

He smiled, though it was small and a little sad. "I'll see you tomorrow?"

"Yeah," she said, trying to smile despite the weight of what had just happened between them. "Tomorrow."

Maya got out of the vehicle and watched it leave to take Ryan back to Mark's, her heart still pounding in her chest. She knew she'd crossed a line tonight—a line that couldn't be uncrossed. Right now, though, she only thought of the feeling of her body pressed against his.

She smiled at the promise in his voice, though. *Tomorrow.* At least that meant he wasn't going to go back to avoiding her.

She made her way inside before she could start to doubt herself, making sure that Shelby had made it home alright, too.

Chapter 18

Ryan's POV

Ryan woke up with a start, the echo of Maya's lips still lingering on his skin. His room was dark, the early morning light barely creeping through the blinds. He sighed, running a hand through his messy hair, his mind stuck on what had almost happened the night before.

He'd pulled away. He had to. But now, lying in the quiet of his room, he wasn't so sure. Every time he closed his eyes, he could feel her pressed against him, her breath warm on his neck, the way she looked up at him just before...

Ryan groaned, turning over, staring at the blank wall. He had tossed and turned all night, trying to push the memory of that moment out of his head. He couldn't shake the feeling that pulling away had been the wrong decision. Maya had made the first move—did that mean she felt the same? Or was it the alcohol? The last thing he had wanted, then or now, was to take advantage of her being in too incapacitated a state to make a consensual choice.

The way her lips felt, the way his body had responded without thinking—he had decided. If they both managed to snag places in New York, he was going to confess his feelings to Maya. Worst case, New York was huge, and he could hide amongst all the people, but best case....

Ryan sat up, pushing the covers off his legs, his head heavy from the restless night. He had to consider the possibility of her getting a job in New York, and him ending up elsewhere, like LA. There was no sense in complicating their lives with something that couldn't go anywhere.

But even as he told himself that, he couldn't stop the flood of images flashing through his mind—Maya, laughing at the bar, her eyes meeting his in that knowing way. The feeling of her body, warm and soft against him. His lips devouring hers again in the back of the car...

Ryan cursed under his breath, contemplating a cold shower.

He needed to get out of his own head, focus on what mattered: his applications, his future, anything to get him through these interviews and earn his place in New York and his place at Maya's side.

But no matter how hard he tried, he couldn't forget the way her lips had felt or the way his heart had raced in a way it never had before.

Ryan cursed under his breath again, rubbing his temples as the sharp throb of a headache pulsed behind his eyes. The hangover was worse than he expected—he hadn't even had that much to drink. It was the stress, he supposed. The late night. The... offer of more.

Stop thinking about it.

With a grunt, he swung his legs over the edge of the bed and stood up, feeling the room spin slightly as he steadied himself. He groaned, running a hand through his hair as he dragged himself to the bathroom. Splashing cold water on his face, he stared at his reflection, bloodshot eyes staring back at him. He looked as messed up as he felt. The night replayed in fragments—Maya's smile, her body against his, and the tension in his gut from pulling away. His body responded to these memories before he could stop it. It was getting painful, trying to suppress these reactions.

How the hell am I supposed to focus on anything right now?

Taking some deep breaths and taking the fastest cold shower ever to calm himself down, he composed himself before the scent of coffee pulled him out of the bathroom. Mark and Emily were already up, the clank of early morning activity coming from the kitchen. He rubbed the back of his neck and made his way out.

Mark was leaning against the counter, mug in hand, while Emily stood by the sink, half focused on her phone. Ryan squinted at the sunlight streaming in through the windows, wincing at the brightness.

"Rough night, man?" Mark asked with a knowing grin, raising his mug in a mock toast.

Ryan grunted in response, reaching for a glass and filling it with water. "You could say that."

Emily looked up, concern flickering in her eyes. "You look like death warmed over. Didn't sleep?"

Ryan shook his head, taking a long drink of water. "Not much. Head's killing me." He caught the curious look Emily shot him, but he wasn't in the mood to explain. Not yet.

Mark chuckled. "That's what happens when you stay out till the wee hours of morning while drinking enough for a small army."

"Yeah, well..." Ryan muttered, setting the glass down and slumping into a chair at the table.

Emily put her phone down and moved toward the coffee maker, pouring a fresh cup. "Here, this might help," she said, handing it to him.

Ryan gave a small smile. "Thanks."

As he took a sip, the rich bitterness cut through the fog in his head, but the tension was still there, coiled tight in his chest. He could feel Emily's eyes on him, studying him.

"What's really going on?" she asked gently, pulling up a chair next to him.

Ryan exhaled slowly, running his fingers through his hair. "Just... thinking about everything."

Mark raised an eyebrow, leaning against the counter again. "You've got interviews lined up, right?"

"Yeah," Ryan said, nodding. "But it's just... overwhelming. Feels like everything's happening all at once, and I'm not sure where I'm gonna land. How are you guys handling all this?" He glanced between Emily and Mark, hoping to steer the conversation away from the mess in his head.

Emily exchanged a quick look with Mark before answering. "I mean, it's a lot, no question about it. I've got some interviews in Chicago, and Mark's got a few in the same area. We've been talking about what's next, but honestly, we're just taking it one step at a time."

Ryan's brow furrowed. "But how are you navigating it together? Like... figuring out if you'll end up in the same place or not? Are you only applying to Chicago? What if one of you were to not find something?"

Emily sighed, her eyes softening. "We've had to be realistic about it. There's no guarantee we'll both end up in the same city, but we're applying to places we think fit us individually first. If we're meant to end up together in the same place, it'll happen. If not... well, we'll cross that bridge when we get to it. Personally, I'm just trying not to put that idea into the universe."

Ryan's mind raced, replaying her words. He couldn't help but think about Maya. No guarantee they'd end up in the same place either. She was looking at firms in New York, but what if he ended up somewhere else? What if they just missed each other entirely? Or what if he had screwed things up by turning her down last night?

Mark chimed in, his tone more practical. "It's stressful, no doubt. But we've got options. I think we both know we have to focus on what's best for us career-wise first. We've had some good talks about it, and we're just staying open to whatever comes next."

Ryan nodded slowly, appreciating their perspective but feeling that familiar churn of uncertainty in his gut.

Mark clapped him on the shoulder, jarring him out of his thoughts. "You'll figure it out, man. You've got some solid options."

Ryan forced a smile. "Yeah, I know. I have faith you two will end up together still, too."

Emily smiled appreciatively at him as she got up to refill her coffee from the nearly empty pot.

But as he finished his own cup, his mind wandered back to Maya again. *If we're meant to end up together...*

He shook his head, trying to push the thought away. It was too much to think about right now.

Shelby's POV

Shelby blinked against the sunlight streaming into the kitchen, her head throbbing faintly from the remnants of last night's drinking. She wasn't nearly as bad off as Maya, but she still felt the dull ache behind her eyes as she impatiently awaited her coffee, hoping the caffeine would work its magic soon.

Maya had yet to emerge from her room, and Shelby couldn't help but smirk at the thought of how wrecked her friend probably felt. The celebration had been worth it, though. All of them landing interviews were a big deal. And besides, it had been a while since they'd all gone out like that.

She flipped through her notes, halfheartedly trying to focus on her work, when she heard Maya's bedroom door creak open. A moment later, Maya shuffled into the kitchen, looking as rough as Shelby had expected. Her hair was a mess, and her oversized t-shirt hung off one shoulder, clearly thrown on in haste.

"Morning," Shelby said, her greeting deliberately light. "How are we feeling?"

Maya made a noise somewhere between a groan and a sigh as she poured herself a cup of coffee. "Ugh."

Shelby chuckled, sitting back in her chair. "I told you those extra shots of tequila were a bad idea."

Maya waved her off, too focused on her coffee to retort. She leaned against the counter, taking small, cautious sips, and Shelby watched her for a moment. There was something different about her today, more than just the hangover. Maya was quiet, like she was deep in thought.

"So," Shelby began, trying to sound casual. "You came in pretty late last night. Everything okay? I didn't think your car was so far behind us. If I hadn't heard you close your door last night, I probably would have been worried you went missing!"

Maya hesitated, her eyes flicking up briefly before settling back on her coffee. "Yeah... I guess."

Shelby raised an eyebrow. "Uh-huh. You guess?"

Maya shifted uncomfortably, her fingers fidgeting with the handle of her mug. "I, uh... I kissed Ryan last night."

Shelby's eyebrows shot up, and she leaned forward in her chair. "You *what*?"

Maya groaned, burying her face in her hands. "I know. It was so stupid. I don't even know why I did it. I thought—well, I don't know what I thought. Maybe I was misreading things or... I don't know."

Shelby's surprise morphed into confusion, though she kept her tone gentle. "Okay, slow down. Start from the beginning. What happened? Why would you have misread things?"

Maya dropped her hands and sighed. "We were just talking at the bar. It felt... nice. I don't know. I had a few drinks, and when we were on the way home in our rideshare, I kissed him."

"And?" Shelby prompted, sensing that there was more to the story.

Maya winced. "And he shut me down."

"Ouch."

"Yeah," Maya muttered, her face flushing with embarrassment. "I feel so stupid. I thought maybe... I don't know what I thought. It just felt like something was there, but I guess I was wrong, and he isn't interested."

Shelby's smile softened. "Hey, don't beat yourself up. You were both drinking, and who knows what was going through his head? It doesn't mean you misread anything. Maybe he was trying to be respectful?"

Maya shook her head. "No, I think I messed up. I don't regret kissing him, exactly. More like, I don't regret putting myself out there. I just... I'm embarrassed now. He stopped me, and I feel like things will be weird now."

Shelby frowned, leaning forward even more. "Maya, listen. You're allowed to feel. You've both been through a lot, and if there was a moment, even if he pulled back, that doesn't mean you were wrong to feel it. Maybe he's just... I don't know, scared? Confused? Just as conflicted as you've been?"

"Maybe," Maya said quietly, fidgeting. "I just don't know how to go forward now or what things will be like."

Shelby reached across the table, giving her hand a reassuring squeeze. "Give it time. If Ryan's as good a guy as we know he is, he'll figure it out."

Maya gave a small nod, though she still looked conflicted. Shelby decided not to push further for now, switching the conversation back to nonsense that didn't require a lot of brain power. She thought about her own situationship and wondered if she would be confident enough to put herself out there like that.

Like Maya, she was looking to the future and knew she would be moving in a few short months, and that life would be drastically changing sooner than she might be ready for.

Chapter 19

Ryan's POV

Ryan's head felt moderately better, the headache now a dull ache rather an all-consuming throbbing. He leaned back in his chair, staring at the pages of his finance textbook without absorbing any of the information. Studying wasn't going to be easy today, but he was determined that he wasn't going to stumble this close to the 'finish line.'

He cursed under his breath for what felt like the hundredth time that morning. Maya had kissed him.

He'd turned her down.

And now he couldn't stop thinking about it.

With a sigh, he grabbed his coffee and took a long sip, trying to shove the memory aside. He had more important things to focus on, like increasing his chances of landing something in New York.

Mark wandered into the living room, looking far more alert than Ryan felt. He raised an eyebrow at Ryan's slouched position at the dining table. "Still struggling?"

Ryan grunted. "Something like that." He suddenly focused on Mark. "You don't have work to do today?"

Mark grabbed a bottle of water from the fridge, leaning against the counter as he cracked it open. "Naw, I got the hard stuff outta the way already so I just have a few smaller tasks that can wait 'til tomorrow. I'm glad I did based on the look of you."

Ryan rubbed his temples. "I hate you."

Mark laughed. "I know. Any more emails for interviews?"

Ryan shrugged, his eyes flicking down to the table. "No, not yet. The more the merrier at this point, though."

Mark's gaze sharpened as if he sensed there was more. "And?"

Ryan hesitated, feeling the weight of last night pressing down on him. He hadn't told anyone yet, but maybe it was time to let something slip. "I kissed Maya last night."

Mark's eyes widened. "Whoa, hold up. You kissed her? Or...?"

Ryan winced. "Okay, she kissed me. But still. We kissed."

Mark whistled, his expression a mix of surprise and curiosity. "Damn. So, what did you do?"

Ryan ran a hand through his hair, the memory of that moment playing in his mind again. "I kissed her back... but then I panicked. I pulled away."

Mark blinked. "Why?"

Ryan sighed, leaning back in his chair. "I don't know. I guess I wasn't sure it was really her and not the alcohol."

Mark nodded slowly. "Okay, I can respect that. If she kissed you again, sober, would you react the same? Or would you let it happen?"

Ryan frowned, his eyes narrowing in thought. "What do you mean?"

Mark shrugged, sipping his water again. "I mean, I get making sure she really wants things to progress, but maybe you pulled away for another reason. It sounds like there's something there, but you're too worried about all the what-ifs."

Ryan didn't respond right away, turning Mark's words over in his mind. Maybe he was right. Waiting to see what kind of job offers came through seemed like the most logical step, but was it really? Did it really matter?

Mark watched Ryan carefully, letting the silence stretch as Ryan fidgeted with his coffee mug. He didn't usually talk about this stuff—not with Mark, not with anyone. But now that it was out there, he couldn't stop the flood of thoughts rushing forward.

"It's not just about the kiss," Ryan said after a moment, quieter now. "There's more to it. That night a few weeks ago, after things with Cole got bad, I... I ended up staying at Maya's place. I slept in her bed."

Mark raised an eyebrow. "Wait, what? You slept in her bed?"

Ryan nodded, his eyes distant as the memory resurfaced. "Yeah. It wasn't like that, though. I mean, I was on the couch at first. But she felt bad, I guess. She offered me her bed, and... I don't know, man. We were just lying there, but it felt different. Like, every time I closed my eyes, I could feel her next to me. It's been in my head ever since."

Mark let out a low whistle. "Damn. You got it bad."

Ryan sighed, rubbing his face with his hands. "Yeah, tell me about it. And now, after last night, I feel like I've wrecked everything. I stopped her after the kiss, and now she probably thinks I don't feel the same. I've been shutting down all these moments between us for so long, and I'm worried I've actually ruined my chance this time."

Mark leaned against the counter, crossing his arms as he considered Ryan's words. "Look, I think that you're overthinking this. But let me give you some food for thought. Beyond the alcohol, what would be stopping you from pursuing her if she wanted it? If you can't answer that, then maybe you don't really have a reason and need to stop kidding yourself."

Ryan groaned, staring at his hands. "I know. I've always kept this wall up when it comes to Maya. She was with Cole, and it just... It never felt right for me to even think about her like that. But lately... I don't know. It's hard to ignore how I feel, but at the same time, I don't want to end up hurting her or getting hurt by starting something and then ending up in different places and things falling apart."

Mark took a sip of his water, his eyes thoughtful. "Man, I get that you're scared, but pulling away isn't going to make those feelings go away. If anything, it's only going to make things worse between you two. You're both walking on eggshells now."

Ryan leaned back in his chair, letting out a frustrated breath. "I know. But I can't help thinking she's going to hate me now. I shut her down, Mark. She kissed me, put herself out there and invited me inside, and I rejected her. How do I come back from that? She's probably thinking I don't want anything to do with her at this point."

Mark's expression softened, and he took a few steps closer, leaning on the back of the chair across from Ryan. "She doesn't hate you, man. You're overthinking this. Trust me, if she kissed you, there's something there. She's probably just as confused as you are right now. You're not the only one who's afraid of messing things up."

Ryan stared into his coffee, his mind swirling with uncertainty. "I don't know, man. I feel like I've been running from this for so long."

Mark tilted his head, considering Ryan's words. "I get that. You both have a lot going on, and there's no guarantee you'll end up in the same place. But honestly? I think you're focusing too much on the 'what-ifs.' You've been friends for years, and you've always had her back. If there's something more between you two, you'll figure it out. Don't write it off just because of logistics. Feelings don't care about being logical."

Ryan slumped in his chair, rubbing his temples as the headache from the hangover seemed to intensify. "Easier said than done. You should have seen the look on her face when I told her it wasn't a good idea. I can't stop seeing that image of her now. I hurt her and need to figure out how to make things right before anything else."

Mark gave him a sympathetic look, his gaze softening. "Then you have to talk to her, man. Just tell her you need to explain and clear the air. The worst thing you can do is avoid it and let it fester. Communicating is always a good first step. If you explain why you pulled away, she'll understand. She knows you—better than most people. She'll get it."

Ryan let out a deep breath, leaning his head back and closing his eyes for a moment. He knew Mark was right. Avoiding Maya wasn't going to fix anything. He needed to talk to her, be honest about what had happened and why he'd reacted the way he had. But the idea of that conversation felt like walking into a storm.

"Yeah, I guess I'll have to," Ryan muttered, though the thought of confronting Maya about last night sent a nervous flutter through his chest. He wasn't ready for that conversation, not yet. But soon he would have to face it.

Mark clapped him on the shoulder, offering a reassuring smile. "You've got this. Just take it one step at a time. And maybe, next time she kisses you, let her."

Ryan huffed out a laugh despite himself. "Yeah, I suppose I'll have to wait and see if she even does."

Mark straightened up, tossing his empty water bottle into the recycling bin. "Oh, she will. You'll figure it out, man."

Ryan nodded. Maybe Mark was right. But now the ball was in his court, and the question was whether he'd have the guts to pick it up and make the next move.

He turned back to his laptop, determination and the fragments of a plan starting to form.

The quiet hum of the library was usually calming for Ryan, but today, it did nothing to soothe the chaos in his head. The soft click of his fingers against the mousepad filled the silence as he scrolled through his notes. His half-empty coffee cup sat neglected beside him, long gone cold. He rubbed the back of his neck, the tension from the other night still coiled tight in his muscles. It had been several days since he had seen Maya and he still hadn't spoken to Cole, either.

His mind wasn't on his work—it hadn't been all morning. Every time he tried to focus, his thoughts drifted back to Maya. The way she'd kissed him, the way she'd walked away. He kept replaying it over and over, trying to build up the courage to message her, to test the waters and sense her reaction to him in the cold light of day.

His phone buzzed on the table, and his heart jumped at the thought of it being her. But when he glanced down, it was just a reminder for an upcoming assignment. He sighed, rubbing his temples as a headache started to build.

The last thing he expected was to see Maya today. He still didn't feel ready for that conversation, not yet. He needed time to figure out what to say and how to say it. But just as the thought crossed his mind, there she was.

From the corner of his eye, he saw her walking toward him. Her hair was pulled up in a loose ponytail, and she had her bag slung over one shoulder, looking a little worse for wear but still beautiful. His pulse quickened, and he forced himself to look down at his laptop, pretending to be absorbed in whatever article was on the screen. Maybe if he focused hard enough, she'd walk past and—

"Hey, Ryan."

He glanced up, his heart doing a weird flip in his chest as she stood in front of him, holding two cups of coffee in her hands.

"Maya," he said, trying to keep his tone steady. "Hey."

She gave him a tentative smile, one that didn't quite reach her eyes, and held out a cup toward him. "Peace offering," she said hesitantly. "I figured you could use a fresh coffee."

He stared at the cup for a moment before taking it from her, his fingers brushing hers in the exchange. The familiar jolt of electricity shot through him at the contact, and he quickly pulled his hand away, setting the cup down on the table. "Thanks," he muttered, unsure of what else to say.

Maya shifted awkwardly, looking almost nervous. She dropped her bag on the chair across from him and sat down, not waiting for an invitation. Ryan tensed, not sure how this conversation was about to play out.

"I wanted to talk to you," she said after a moment. "About the other night."

Ryan swallowed, his mouth suddenly dry. He'd known this conversation was coming, but it didn't make it any easier. "You don't have to—" he started, but she cut him off.

"No, I do." She sighed, tucking a loose strand of hair behind her ear. "I... I feel like I put you in a weird position, and I'm really sorry for that. I never wanted to compromise our friendship or make things awkward between us."

He frowned, leaning back in his chair. "You didn't—"

"Yes, I did," she interrupted again, her eyes full of regret. "I kissed you, and I acted in a way that I shouldn't have. I know things are complicated, with Cole and... everything. I shouldn't have put you in that situation."

Ryan's chest tightened at the mention of Cole's name. He had no idea how to respond, how to tell her that it wasn't the kiss itself that was the problem, but everything that came with it. The future he could see and desperately wanted but didn't know would be possible.

"Maya, it wasn't your fault," he said finally. "I just... I wasn't thinking, and in trying not to take advantage of you after drinking, I reacted badly. I didn't mean to make you feel like you did something wrong."

Maya paused, her fingers fidgeting with the strap of her bag. "I just don't want this to change things between us. You're important to me, Ryan. I don't want to lose that because I acted on impulse."

Ryan exhaled slowly, running a hand through his hair. He understood where she was coming from, but the truth was, things had already changed. There was no undoing the tension that had been building between them, not after that kiss, not after everything. But he didn't want to make her feel like she was the only one dealing with it.

"You're not going to lose me, Maya," he said. "We've been through too much for that. I wanted it, too, I just... I don't know what's going to happen in the next few months and I don't want to start something that could hurt you. Hurt us both if it ended badly."

Maya's eyes flickered up to meet his, and for a moment, the vulnerability between them was palpable. "I don't either," she admitted, so quietly he almost didn't hear. "But I don't regret it, Ryan. I don't regret kissing you. I just wish I hadn't made you feel like you had to choose right now. I want you in my life, regardless of what that relationship might be."

Ryan's heart skipped a beat at her words, and he looked away, the familiar swirl of affection and anxiety rising in his chest. He didn't regret it either—not the kiss, not the feelings he'd been harboring for weeks.

"I just think we need to see where we land with these interviews," he said with a steadiness he hadn't realized he was capable of in this moment. "I don't regret it, either, other than my reaction, but I would also never want to make you choose somewhere outside of New York when you've worked so hard for that dream. My pessimistic side also doesn't want to rush into something and make things worse because we're across the country and long-distance relationships suck."

Maya nodded, though her eyes seemed sadder now. "I understand. I just... wanted you to know that I'm sorry. For everything. And that I care about you. A lot."

Ryan's throat tightened, and he forced himself to nod. "I care about you too, Maya. I really do. I don't want you to have regrets."

She stood then, slinging her bag over her shoulder, her expression resigned. "I'll let you get back to work. But if you ever want to talk... I'm here. And... I hope we both end up in NYC."

Ryan watched as she walked away, the tension in his chest relaxing after having that conversation. At least she didn't hate him. He took a sip of the coffee she'd brought him, calm spreading through his body. All he knew was that every time he closed his eyes, he could still feel the ghost of her kiss. And he would count down to them both being in New York.

A few hours later, he walked down the steps of the library, the cool evening air biting at his skin. He balanced his phone between his ear and shoulder while he made his way to his car parked on the street. His brother's voice crackled over the line, filling the silence of his walk, going on about his family and wife.

"So, the kids are good?" Ryan asked, smiling as he heard his nephew yelling in the background.

"Good? They're absolute terrors," his brother, Tyler, said with a laugh. "Maggie had a meltdown in the middle of the grocery store yesterday. Full-on screaming, snot everywhere. And Jake, well, he's going through that phase where he doesn't want to wear pants anymore. Just wants to run around in his underwear like a superhero."

Ryan chuckled, shaking his head as he pictured his niece and nephew. "Sounds like they're keeping you on your toes."

"Yeah, no kidding. But hey, I wouldn't trade it for anything," Tyler said, and Ryan relaxed at the normalcy of their conversation. "They're great kids. Speaking of family, you're still coming to Emma's wedding this summer, right?"

Ryan opened his car door and slid into the driver's seat, the familiar scent of old leather greeting him. "Of course. No way I'm missing it. How's everything going with that, anyway?"

"Stressful," Tyler replied with a groan. "Mom's been driving her insane with wedding details. But you know Em, she's keeping it together, making sure everything's perfect and running smoothly as always."

Ryan smiled as he started the car, the engine rumbling to life. "That sounds like her. She's always been the organized one."

"Yep. Meanwhile, I just have to show up, give my speech, and hope I don't screw it up too badly."

Ryan laughed, pulling out onto the road. The drive back to Mark's was generally pretty quick, but talking to his brother made him want to take his time. "You'll do fine. You've always been better at the whole 'adulting' thing than I am, anyway."

Tyler snorted. "Not sure about that. But hey, I've got a wife, two kids, and a mortgage—so I guess that qualifies me."

Ryan grinned, feeling a sense of pride for his brother. He admired how Tyler had built his life, balancing family and work with a sense of ease. It was something Ryan aspired to, even if he wasn't there yet.

"So," Tyler said after a beat, his tone shifting to something more serious. "What's going on with you? Mom said you're looking at jobs in New York?"

"Yeah," Ryan replied, a sigh escaping him. "Got a couple interviews lined up there. New York, LA, Chicago and of course home in Hartford, too. I'm trying to keep my options open, though."

"That's awesome, man. You'll crush it. New York's a hell of a lot closer than you are now, too, so maybe we'd get to see you more than a few times a year. But... why do I feel like there's more going on?"

Ryan hesitated, gripping the steering wheel a little tighter. He hadn't told Tyler the whole story yet, hadn't talked much about the mess with Cole or the complicated feelings swirling around Maya. But if anyone could give him solid advice, it was his brother.

"Things have been... complicated," Ryan admitted. "It's Cole. And Maya."

There was a pause on the other end before Tyler spoke again, his tone curious but not pushing. "What happened?"

Ryan took a deep breath, feeling the weight of everything he'd been holding onto. "Cole and I... we had a fight. He's been a mess since he and Maya broke up last year. I've been trying to stay out of it, but... things with Maya, they've changed. We've gotten closer, and I think that I have real feelings for her now. It's driven a wedge between Cole and I, though."

Tyler was silent for another moment, letting Ryan's words hang in the air before he responded. "You and Maya, huh?"

"Yeah," Ryan said, feeling the familiar tension ramp up at her name. "I've always cared about her as a friend. Now, though, things are changing, and it just turned into a mess when Cole got physical with her. I couldn't let that go."

Tyler let out a thoughtful hum. "Look, I get that it's messy. Cole's your friend, and there's history there, but you can't keep putting yourself last because of it. If Maya's the one you want to be with, you need to figure that out. I think you did the right thing standing up for her and calling him out for being a shit human, and I'm glad you did. Cole will either have to accept it or not, but that's not your responsibility. He has to make that decision and live with the consequences. Unfortunately, that may mean your friendship doesn't survive, but that part is a risk you'll need to take if you're serious about Maya."

Ryan sighed, the truth in his brother's words hitting him harder than he'd expected. He knew Tyler was right—he had already made his decision that Maya was worth that risk of ruining his friendship with Cole. Honestly, even if he hadn't developed these feelings, seeing the person that Cole had become who put his hands on a woman might have ended their friendship anyway.

"Maya's applying in New York, too. I know she's worth losing Cole's friendship, but what if we don't even land jobs in the same place?" Ryan asked tightly. "I'm not sure about starting something that immediately becomes long-distance or ends."

"You might not," Tyler said honestly. "But if it's worth it, and I mean really worth it, it'll work out in the end. You'll both just need to put in the work to keep that alive. Relationships *are* work. And even if things end... well, you have to live your life, Ryan. You can't keep putting everything on hold for other people. You deserve to be happy, too, even just in this moment. You can't worry about a future that might not even happen."

Ryan nodded, even though Tyler couldn't see him. "I guess."

"And Maya," Tyler continued, "It sounds like she cares about you, man. You don't pull away from someone like that unless you're scared of what it means. So, don't let fear hold you back. If Maya's still what you want, go for it."

Ryan swallowed hard, his mind racing. He thought about the way Maya had kissed him, the way it had felt to pull away when every part of him wanted to stay in that moment. Tyler was right—he couldn't keep running from this.

"Maybe you're right. I think I owe Cole a conversation about everything, but then Maya deserves better than waiting around to see what happens." Ryan said finally, feeling a sense of resolution settling over him.

"Good," Tyler replied. "And hey, you've got us in Hartford if you need a break from it all. The kids would love to see their Uncle Ryan."

Ryan smiled at the thought of his niece and nephew, his heart warming. "I'll see you all soon, I promise."

"Hold you to that," Tyler said with a chuckle. "Take care of yourself, Ry. And don't overthink it too much. Sometimes you just have to let things happen."

Ryan hung up a few minutes later, his heart feeling a little lighter after the conversation. Tyler always had a way of making things seem simpler, of cutting through the noise and focusing on what really mattered.

Ryan exhaled slowly. He knew what he needed to do. Making an impulsive decision, he cut down a side road, changing direction. He needed to have this conversation with Cole before he stopped himself.

Chapter 20

Cole's POV

Cole lounged back on the couch, a half-empty beer bottle in his hand, staring blankly at the TV. Beside him, Jen—someone he'd met a few nights ago at a bar—curled up under his arm, scrolling through her phone. He liked her well enough, but she was mostly a distraction, a way to forget about the constant churn of anger and regret that had been gnawing at him for damn near a year now.

He took another swig of his beer, trying to drown out the image of Maya that always seemed to linger at the back of his mind. She was everywhere: every corner of this apartment reminded him of her, even though this was a different apartment than they had shared together. He tried to tell himself that he was over her, that it was Maya's fault they had fallen apart, but the truth was harder to swallow.

Before he could lose himself too much in his thoughts, the sound of the front door opening pulled him out of his haze. Cole glanced up, frowning as Ryan walked in, his expression stormy.

Ryan stopped just inside the doorway, his eyes flicking to Jen before settling on Cole with a look that made Cole absolutely furious. He sat up straighter as the easygoing facade slipped away.

"Ryan? What the hell are you doing here?" Cole asked, immediately defensive.

Ryan closed the door behind him, his jaw tight. "We need to talk."

Cole's heart picked up, knowing exactly what this was about. He'd been avoiding this conversation for too long, but he wasn't ready to deal with it now, especially not with Jen sitting beside him, blissfully unaware of the reason for the tension thickening the air.

Jen shifted, feeling the change in Cole's posture. "Uh, maybe I should—"

"Yeah, you should go," Ryan said, cutting her off without even looking at her.

Cole winced at the bluntness of it, but he didn't argue. Jen gave him an awkward smile before sliding off the couch and grabbing her things. The sound of her leaving felt like a heavy weight settling in the room.

As soon as the door clicked shut behind her, Cole looked back at Ryan, whose eyes were blazing. "You're such a hypocrite."

Cole blinked, taken aback by Ryan's venom. "What the hell are you talking about?"

Ryan stepped forward, his hands clenching into fists at his sides. "You've been giving me hell about Maya for months, accusing me of things that never even happened, while you're out here with someone new? And she's not the first since Maya, either. Yet you've got the nerve to act like you're the victim in all this?"

Cole shot up from the couch, his own anger flaring. "Don't you dare. You don't get to come in here and judge me, Ryan. You've been sneaking around with Maya behind my back, pretending to be my friend when—"

"We never snuck around!" Ryan interrupted sharply. "Nothing happened between me and Maya until recently, and even then, *I* pulled away because *I* didn't want to hurt you. But you're making this impossible!"

Cole's hands clenched, his chest tightening as Ryan's words hit him. Ryan and Maya? Something really happened? He wanted to argue, wanted to throw something back in Ryan's face, to rant a rave about how he has been right, had *known* there were feeling there. Another part of him, though, deep down, knew Ryan was probably telling the truth and it was only a recent development.

"You don't get it, Ryan," Cole said lower now, his anger giving way to something more vulnerable. "You don't understand what it's like to watch the person you thought you'd spend the rest of your life with... change. Maya and I had a plan, we had everything mapped out. Then she starts talking about moving to New York, about not wanting a family. That wasn't the plan. She wasn't the same person anymore."

Ryan shook his head, his gaze softening just a little. "No, Cole. She didn't change; she just finally put herself first. That's not her fault. And it's not yours, either. But you can't keep blaming her for not fitting into the box that you put her in. And that will never excuse you putting your hand on her."

Cole winced at the truth of it, feeling exposed. He ran a hand through his hair, pacing the small living room. "I didn't mean to hurt her," he muttered, barely audible. "But that doesn't make it any better that she all but lied to me for... who even knows how long. And now? Moving on with someone who has been my best friend for years? That's just cold-hearted."

Ryan exhaled, clearly frustrated but trying to keep calm. "And I never meant for this to happen. I swear. But... I care about her. I'm not going to keep pretending like I don't."

Cole stopped in his tracks, turning to face Ryan. The weight of everything crashed down on him—the realization that he'd been holding on to something that wasn't ever going to be. Maya didn't want the same things as him, and maybe she never had.

"So what? You're going to be with her now?" Cole asked, not even trying to hide his jealousy.

Ryan didn't answer immediately. He looked conflicted, as though he wasn't sure himself. "I don't know," he admitted finally. "But I can't lie to myself about how I feel anymore. And I need to know where you stand, because I'm tired of all this... fighting. If something happens between me and Maya, I don't want your shadow looming over us."

Cole stood there, feeling the last of his anger draining away, leaving only exhaustion in its wake. He thought back to all the times he and Maya had fought, all the moments when he realized they weren't seeing eye to eye anymore. Maybe it had been over long before they officially ended things, and maybe, just maybe, Maya was better off with someone who understood her in ways he couldn't.

"I don't know what to say, man," Cole said, slumping back onto the couch. "Part of me feels like you've betrayed me, but... maybe you're right. Maybe she didn't change. Maybe she just wasn't the person I wanted her to be."

Ryan stayed quiet, watching Cole with a mixture of sympathy and frustration. "Look, I don't want to lose you as a friend. But I'm not going to sit around pretending things are fine when they're not. You need to decide what's more important: holding onto something that's already broken or moving forward and finding happiness."

Cole dropped his head into his hands, rubbing his temples. He wasn't in the best mind space to figure this out, not after the beers he'd drank tonight. He did know that he was tired of being angry, though, and tired of feeling alone.

"Just... give me some time," Cole muttered roughly. "I need to figure this out."

Ryan nodded, accepting that for now. "Take whatever time you need, man. Let me know if you want to talk again."

Cole didn't respond, just sat there, feeling the weight of his anger sliding away. He might feel different in the light of morning, but right now, he just wanted to move on.

Ryan lingered for a moment longer before finally turning to leave. As the door closed behind him, Cole leaned his head back against the couch, staring up at the ceiling. His mind swirled with everything that had just been said, and for the first time in months, he allowed himself to envision life moving on without Maya in it.

Chapter 21

Maya's POV

The air felt different today—lighter, warmer. The sun had finally decided to show up after weeks of clouds, and Maya couldn't stop herself from smiling as she stepped out of her apartment. The birds were chirping in the trees and the breeze that brushed her face carried with it the promise of new beginnings.

She pulled her jacket tighter around herself out of habit, even though she knew it wouldn't be necessary much longer. There were only a few weeks left until graduation, and with her interviews finally behind her, it felt like the future she'd been working toward for so long was just within reach.

The interview process had been exhausting, but every time she thought about the possibilities waiting for her in the city, excitement bubbled up in her chest. She felt like she'd aced the ones that mattered most—the ones with firms she could actually see herself working for, living in the city she'd always dreamed about. By the end of the month, she'd know whether she had secured a place at one of them. The thought made her heart clench.

Her mind was already in New York. She could almost picture herself there—walking down busy streets, coffee in hand, racing to a job that actually excited her. It was everything she'd wanted for herself. Everything she had imagined, even if there was still uncertainty about what life might look like once she got there.

As she wandered through campus, lost in thought, a familiar voice pulled her out of her daydreams. "Maya."

She turned, her eyes widening when she saw Cole walking toward her. She hadn't seen him since that awkward encounter at the café. Her gut twisted at the memory of their argument, the tight grip he'd had on her arm, the bruise that had lingered far too long.

Maya's instinct was to avoid him, to walk away and pretend she hadn't heard, but something in his expression stopped her. He didn't look angry. In fact, he looked... calm.

"Cole," she greeted cautiously. "Hey."

He stopped in front of her, shoving his hands into his pants pockets, his gaze flicking between her and the ground. "I've been meaning to talk to you," he said, his tone quieter than usual. "About... everything."

Maya's heart rate quickened. She wasn't sure where this conversation was going, but curiosity won out. "Okay."

Cole shifted on his feet, looking as uncomfortable as she felt. "Look, I know things between us ended pretty messily," he began, taking a deep breath. "And I've been carrying around a lot of anger, thinking you were the one who changed, thinking it was your fault things didn't work out. But I realize now that's not fair."

Maya blinked, taken aback by his words. This was not how she'd expected this conversation to go. "Cole..."

"Please, let me finish," he interrupted, holding up a hand. "I've had a lot of time to think, and after talking to Ryan, I realized that maybe we just wanted different things but I was a poor boyfriend and didn't really hear you when you tried to express that. I kept trying to fit us into this plan I had in my head, but... that wasn't fair to you. Or to me."

Maya's breath caught at the mention of Ryan's name. "You talked to Ryan?"

Cole nodded, his expression hardening for a moment before softening again. "Yeah. We had it out a few days ago. And... I'm not going to lie, Maya, it still stings. I don't know if I'll ever be completely on board with seeing you two together, but... I can't keep holding it against you for not being the person I wanted you to be. That person isn't you, and that's okay. You deserve happiness with whomever you find it with."

Maya stared at him, trying to process everything. Cole was letting go. After months of anger, of lashing out, he was finally letting her go. Her heartbeat picked up some more as she processed his words. Ryan and her together? What had Ryan told him?

"I appreciate that, Cole," she said carefully, "I never wanted to hurt you."

"I know." He glanced away, rubbing the back of his neck. "But here's the thing... I can't stand the idea of you and Ryan together. I know it's not rational, but it just... it messes with my head. So, maybe it's best if we keep our distance for a while. At least until I can get my head on straight."

Maya froze. While she didn't regret it, she was not anticipating the discussion of kissing another man with her ex.

"I—" She faltered, a knot forming in her throat. "I didn't know you two talked about so much."

Cole gave her a tight smile. "Yeah, well. It was overdue." He took a step back, shoving his hands deeper into his pockets. "Anyway, I just wanted to let you know that I'm done trying to force your hand. We both deserve to move on."

Maya nodded, her chest tightening. "Thank you, Cole. I... I hope you find what makes you happy."

He gave her one last nod before turning and walking away, leaving her standing there in the warm sun, feeling like the ground had just shifted beneath her.

As the shock wore off, her mind went into overdrive. Ryan had talked to Cole. He had told him... what, exactly? Was it just about them being friends again, or had Ryan confessed that he had feelings for Maya?

She exhaled, pushing her hand through her hair as she tried to calm the storm of thoughts. She didn't have time to dwell on this. There were still two more interviews to get through, and she needed to keep her focus on them. On her future. Yet, she couldn't help but wonder if she and Ryan were now standing on a precipice, waiting for one of them to jump.

Maya hadn't planned to run into Cole. She hadn't planned to feel so unsettled afterward either. Walking briskly across campus, she shook off the conversation, determined not to let it get to her. What mattered right now was finishing the semester strong and preparing for what came next.

Ahead, she spotted Carly sitting on a low wall outside the lecture hall, her usual coffee in hand, legs crossed, looking completely at ease despite everything. She waved when she saw Maya approach.

"Hey!" Carly called out, flashing a bright smile. "I grabbed an extra coffee in case you needed it."

Maya smiled, grateful for the gesture. She could use the caffeine, and the cup felt grounding as she wrapped her hands around it. "You read my mind. Thanks, Carly."

They walked inside together, weaving through students hurrying to their seats. The buzz of conversations about final projects, papers, and upcoming plans filled the air, creating a frantic energy that matched the racing thoughts in Maya's mind.

"So, you hear word yet on any of the interviews you've had so far?" Carly asked as they slid into their usual seats near the back. "I know you were super pumped about them."

Maya sipped her coffee, trying to tamp down the nerves that bubbled up whenever she thought about those interviews. "No, not yet. It's kind of terrifying that everything is just weeks away from being in place and all of us moving on to a new chapter in life, though."

Carly nodded, her expression softening with understanding. "Yeah, it's a lot to process. I've still got a few more interviews myself, but Portland is looking more and more like it's happening." She paused, glancing at Maya with a small smile. "It's funny, right? We've spent all this time here, building toward this, and now that it's finally happening, it's like... what's next?"

Maya sighed, her fingers tracing the edge of her coffee cup. "Exactly. I feel like time is so warped that it's happening so fast and so slowly at the same time. Graduation, job offers... it's all exciting, but I can't shake this thought that I've been planning for this moment for so long, but now that it's here, I don't know what it will actually look like."

Carly gave her a thoughtful look. "I get that. It's kind of like standing at the edge of a cliff, right? You've been climbing and climbing, and now you're at the top, and the only thing left to do is jump. But you don't know where you're going to land."

Maya smiled at Carly's metaphor. "Exactly. What if we jump and it doesn't work out? What if New York isn't what I imagined?"

"What if it's better?" Carly countered, her tone optimistic. "We've put in the work, Maya. You aced those interviews. Any of those firms would be crazy not to hire you. But even if they don't, you've got other options. You're going to land somewhere great. We both are."

Maya smiled, appreciating Carly's unwavering confidence. She wasn't wrong—they had both been working towards this for so long, and no matter how daunting it felt, she had to trust that she'd done everything she could. Either New York would work out or it wouldn't but at least she wouldn't be left wondering about how things could have been different.

"Yeah, you're right," Maya agreed, trying to take deep breaths. "I just need to focus on what I can control and not spiral about the rest of it."

Carly bumped her shoulder lightly. "You got this. Besides, it's not like we're getting thrown out there completely alone. You've got a whole crew to back you up. Whether you end up in New York or not, we'll figure it out together."

Maya smiled, feeling a little more at ease. Carly's words were comforting in a way that Maya hadn't even realized she needed. It wasn't just about landing the job: it was also about knowing she had a support system no matter where she ended up. "Thanks, Carly. That means a lot. And, of course, I hope you know the same goes for you, too."

"No problem." Carly's expression shifted, a teasing grin appearing. "So, I have to ask—how's everything with Ryan?"

Maya nearly choked on her coffee at the sudden shift in conversation. She hadn't told Carly much about what had happened the other night. She wasn't sure how to explain the mix of excitement and embarrassment that had come from kissing Ryan and then watching him pull away.

"Uh..." Maya glanced away, feeling heat creep up her neck. "That's... a situation."

"Oh, come on, don't leave me hanging!" Carly laughed, leaning in. "I know something happened. You've been weird ever since that night."

Maya let out a long breath, deciding there was no point in hiding it any longer. Somehow, she had been able to successfully change the topic any time something a little too close came up, but she knew she needed to come clean. Carly would drag it out of her eventually, anyway. "Okay, fine. I kissed him and invited him inside. And he turned me down."

Carly's eyes widened. "Wait, what? You kissed him? Who *are* you?"

"After the bar the other weekend. We were in the car together, and I don't know... it just happened. But then he rejected me about coming inside and so I ended up stalking him at the library a few days later and apologizing."

Carly frowned, leaning back in her chair. "I don't know, Maya. You really think you misread things? I've seen the way Ryan looks at you."

Maya groaned, running a hand through her hair. "I don't know what to think. I don't regret that I kissed him, but now I just feel like I was pushing him into something he wasn't ready for."

Carly shook her head. "Well, Ryan's not the kind of guy to kiss someone just for the hell of it. He doesn't generally have casual relationships. Maybe he just freaked out about it because of Cole?"

Maya laughed. "Speaking of Cole..."

Carly raised an eyebrow, instantly intrigued. "Oh no, what now?"

"I ran into him on my way here," Maya admitted, rubbing the back of her neck. "It was the strangest thing. He actually apologized. Well, kind of. He said he wasn't going to keep holding things against me, but he also said he can't stand to see me with Ryan, so it's probably best we just keep our distance."

Carly blinked in surprise. "Are we in an alternate reality? *Cole* apologized?"

Maya nodded, still processing the encounter herself. "Yeah, that's what I thought too. I wasn't expecting it at all. He even said he and Ryan talked, which really shocked me. I didn't know they'd had a conversation, but I guess they're working to smooth things over. I'm not sure exactly what Ryan said to him, but it makes me a little nervous."

"Hold on," Carly said, leaning in closer, her voice dropping. "So not only did Ryan and Cole talk, like, for real, but Ryan managed to get Cole to apologize? After all that drama? *And* said something that makes Cole think you guys are together or about to be?"

"I guess so," Maya said, still in disbelief herself. "I don't know all the details, but from what Cole said, it sounds like they might've settled things. I don't know if that's actually true, but he seemed... different. Calmer. Less bitter."

Carly leaned back in her chair, crossing her arms. "Wow. That's... a lot. So, what does that mean for you and Ryan? Ryan must have said something about the two of you for Cole to jump to you guys being together."

Maya shrugged, feeling a mix of relief and uncertainty. "Honestly? I don't know. I'm glad Cole's not holding a grudge anymore, but I'm still trying to wrap my head around it. It sounds like he's finally moving on, and part of me is relieved, but the other part is just... conflicted? Like I don't know if I should be nervous this is some sort of ploy. He seemed pretty genuine, though."

Carly studied her for a moment, her expression thoughtful. "You think Ryan really got him to see that he and you are not a good fit anymore?"

Maya hesitated before answering. "Maybe. I mean, he outright admitted that we should keep our distance because he can't handle seeing me with Ryan, so... yeah. It's weird. It's like he's letting go, but I don't know if that means he's really okay with everything, or if he's just... tired of fighting."

Carly exhaled, her gaze softening. "Well, that's a pretty big step. I mean, for Cole to even say that? Maybe he really is trying to move on. Maybe it doesn't matter why, just that he is."

"Yeah," Maya agreed quietly. "You know, I've wanted closure with him for so long, and now that it feels like we're finally there, I just... I don't know. I expected to feel a weight lift off, not to feel so bad for him."

Carly nodded. "I get it. Reality can be way off from how we thought it would be."

"Exactly," Maya said, shaking her head. "Still, it's kinda freeing. Like, maybe now I can focus on what I really want, instead of worrying about Cole showing up all the time."

Carly smiled knowingly. "And what do you really want?"

Maya's thoughts immediately flickered back to Ryan, the kiss, and everything that had followed. "Well, Ryan, that is, if he's interested." she admitted softly.

Chapter 22

Maya's POV

The campus was quiet at this hour, the usual rush of students long gone, leaving only the occasional footsteps and the rustling of wind through bare tree branches. Maya pulled her scarf tighter around her neck as she stepped out of the library, relieved to finally be heading home.

Then she saw him.

Ryan stood just a few feet away, leaning against the low stone wall that lined the library steps. His phone screen cast a dim glow over his face, his expression unreadable. But the way his thumb hovered over the screen, the slight furrow in his brow—he was hesitating.

Maya slowed her pace, curiosity pricking at her. Ryan wasn't the indecisive type.

"Deep in thought, Taylor?" she called out, breaking the silence.

Ryan startled slightly, his gaze flicking up to hers before he locked his phone and stuffed it into his jacket pocket. "Something like that," he muttered.

Maya arched a brow. "You had the same look on your face before exams. What's up?"

Ryan hesitated, then sighed, rubbing a hand over his jaw. "I got two incredible offers."

Maya tilted her head, confused. "That's great."

He didn't look convinced.

A strange feeling settled over her as she studied him. "Okay, let me guess—you got one back home in Hartford and one in New York?"

Ryan exhaled a short laugh. "Yeah. Pretty much."

Maya nodded, stuffing her hands into her hoodie pocket. She wasn't surprised. Ryan was steady, reliable. Of course, he'd be drawn to Hartford. It was a safe choice, no doubt, with his family there and where his career path would be clear. But the fact that he was hesitating...

"That's not really a choice, is it?" she said.

Ryan shot her a look. "Isn't it?"

Maya shrugged, debating what to say.

"Go on." Ryan encouraged, "I want to hear your thoughts."

Maya shifted her weight against the wall by him. "I mean, yeah, Hartford's comfortable, but New York—it's bigger. It's where everything happens. And if you're even thinking about it, doesn't that mean part of you wants it?"

Ryan let out a slow breath, gaze drifting back to the sidewalk. "New York is... a lot. It's fast-paced, competitive. Everything would be different."

"Yeah," Maya said quietly, "but different isn't always bad. You applied for a reason, right? And the offer wouldn't have been extended if they didn't think you were a great fit. Other than being close to family, do you have a specific reason to want to be in Hartford?"

Ryan's lips pressed together, and Maya could tell he was working through something in his head. A week or so ago, she might've assumed he'd stay in Hartford without a second thought. But now? The fact that he was hesitating—that he was struggling with this choice—felt like something else entirely.

She nudged his arm lightly, forcing a small smile. "You know, for someone in risk management, you're really bad at handling your own risks."

Ryan let out a breathy chuckle, shaking his head. "Yeah, well. It's different when it's your own future."

Maya studied him for a second longer, her heart doing something annoying in her chest. She knew why she cared so much—why the thought of him staying in Hartford felt... wrong. She also didn't want to be the sole reason for any choice he ultimately made.

She swallowed that thought.

Instead, she took a step back, flashing him a teasing grin. "Let me know when you decide to take a risk for once."

Ryan met her gaze, something unreadable flickering behind his eyes. His mouth twitched like he wanted to say something—like he almost did.

But then he just nodded. "Yeah," he said quietly. "I will."

Maya turned and walked away, not daring to look back.

"I'll see you this weekend." She heard him call out suddenly.

She laughed. "Better believe it!"

THE BOWLING ALLEY BUZZED with energy, the sound of clattering pins mixing with laughter and the occasional clink of glasses. Everyone was in good spirits, celebrating the wave of job offers that had started coming in as graduation loomed closer. Even though not all of them had heard back from their top choices yet, it felt like the hard part—getting through years of school—was finally paying off.

Ryan sat across from her, focused on the screen showing their scores. He still seemed to be undecided with his choice between New York and Hartford, but Maya was sure he would figure it out soon. Andrew, Brandon, and Emily were practically glowing from their own good news, each with solid offers lined up. Carly had landed a position she'd been dreaming about for months, and she was still riding the high of knowing she'd be starting her post-grad life on a strong foot.

Mark, on the other hand, was trying to stay optimistic. He hadn't heard back from the one place he really wanted yet, but he'd gotten a few backup offers to fall back on. Still, Maya could tell he was happy, knowing he and Emily would be in Chicago together after all.

As for her, she'd also heard back from some backup firms but was still waiting for her top two choices—Hayes & Martin and Wexler & Greene. She was doing her best to stay positive, but the waiting was gnawing at her.

The game paused as everyone gathered around the table for a quick toast. Carly raised her drink, a wide smile on her face. "Here's to surviving! Offers or not, we did it!"

"To surviving!" they all echoed, clinking their drinks together. Maya forced herself to smile and raise her glass, though her nerves still hummed beneath the surface.

As the others laughed and chatted, Maya's phone buzzed in her pocket. Her heart leapt into her throat as she saw the email notification from *Hayes & Martin.*

Her body practically vibrated as she swiped to open the email. Her fingers hovered over the screen, anticipation making her pulse race. She had to know. She took a deep breath and tapped to open it.

We regret to inform you that due to unforeseen budget constraints, Hayes & Martin will not be hiring at this time.

The words hit her like a punch to the gut. She blinked, staring at the screen, willing the words to change. But they didn't. Hayes & Martin—her dream firm—wasn't hiring. Everything she'd worked for, the interviews, the portfolio... none of it mattered now.

Her vision blurred, and she quickly wiped her eyes. She couldn't lose it here, not in front of everyone. They were celebrating. No one else needed to know how much this sucked, not right now.

Maya stood abruptly, mumbling something about needing a minute, and slipped away from the table. Her legs felt shaky as she made her way toward the hallway near the restrooms. She leaned against the wall, the noise from the bowling alley fading into the background as she tried to steady her breathing.

Suddenly, she felt like a fool. Her mom had cautioned her, but Maya had felt so certain that this firm was where her future lay. So certain that her hard work would pay off and she would end up proving any doubts wrong. So confident she'd be able to get into her top choices just because she worked hard.

It was too much. The waiting, the pressure, the endless guessing about what came next. She had other offers, sure, but Hayes & Martin had been her dream for years. And now, just like that, it was gone.

Her hands trembled as she stared at her phone, unable to focus. The tears came unbidden, some slipping down her cheeks before she could stop them.

"Maya?"

She hadn't heard Ryan approach, but his intonation was soft, full of concern. She didn't want him to see her like this, but she couldn't bring herself to move.

"I just... I needed a minute," she said quietly, wiping her cheeks.

Ryan didn't say anything at first. He stepped closer, and when she finally glanced at him, his expression was so full of understanding that it broke something inside her. Another tear slipped out, and then another, and before she could stop herself, she was crying in earnest.

Without a word, Ryan pulled her into his arms. The embrace was solid, warm, and exactly what she needed. For a moment, Maya froze, but then she let herself sink into it, the tears flowing freely now. She buried her face in his chest, clinging to the comfort of his presence.

"I'm sorry," she murmured through her tears. "I didn't want to make a scene."

Ryan's grip tightened around her, his hand resting gently on the back of her head. "Don't apologize. It's okay."

"It's just... Hayes & Martin." Her voice broke as she said the name. "They're not hiring anymore."

Ryan stayed silent for a moment, his hand stroking her back in slow, soothing circles. "That's really rough, Maya. I'm sorry."

His words, simple as they were, carried a weight that helped ease some of the pressure in her chest. He didn't offer empty reassurance or tell her it didn't matter—he just acknowledged the pain. And that was enough.

Maya sniffed, pulling back slightly so she could look up at him. "Thank you," she whispered hoarsely. "For being here."

Ryan gave her a small smile, though there was something almost sad in his eyes. "You don't have to thank me."

She shook her head and wiped her cheeks. "No, I do. For everything. You've been really good to me... with everything going on. Even with Cole."

Ryan's expression tightened at the mention of Cole, but he didn't pull away.

"He told me you talked," Maya added, searching his face. "I didn't know you two were... working it out."

Ryan let out a slow breath, his jaw clenched. "Well, we talked. I suppose it's still to be seen how things go from there."

Maya pursed her lips, unsure what to say next. She could still feel the weight of his arms around her, the tension between them lingering in the air. "I know things have been weird... but I owe you for talking to him. For smoothing things over."

Ryan shook his head, his grip on her arms firm but gentle. "You don't owe me. Not for that. Not for anything."

There was an intensity in his tone that made her pause, her breath catching in her throat. She stared up at him, suddenly aware of how close they were, of the way his hands rested on her arms, steady and sure.

"I mean it," he added, and she was thrown off by his intensity. "You don't owe me a damn thing."

Maya swallowed, her heart hammering in her chest. The weight of everything—the job rejection, her feelings for Ryan, the uncertainty of their future—hung between them, heavy and unspoken. And yet, in that moment, she wasn't scared or embarrassed. She was just... grateful. For him, for being here, for being her friend, for everything.

"Thank you," she whispered again, barely audible. "For being you, then."

Ryan's lips curved into a faint smile, his gaze never leaving hers. "Anytime."

Ryan's POV

Ryan held Maya in his arms for a moment longer, feeling the tension slowly leave her body. As she took a steadying breath, he loosened his grip, though he stayed close, unwilling to step away just yet. He watched her wipe the last of her tears, her face a mix of sadness and determination as she tried to pull herself back together.

"Ready to head back?" he asked quietly, not wanting to rush her.

Maya nodded, still a little shaky but putting on a brave face. "Yeah, I think so. I needed that."

Ryan gave her a soft smile. "Anytime. Seriously."

She smiled back, though it didn't quite reach her eyes, and he knew that despite her best efforts, the news was still weighing heavily on her. Still, he wasn't going to push her to share it with the others until she was ready. It was her moment, her choice to tell them—or not.

He felt guilt and confusion swirl in him, though he tried to shove it aside for Maya's sake. He had shared his news of offers he received and was conflicted about and now Maya was getting rebuffed by the place he had known she had desperately been counting on. He felt like a fool for throwing his indecision at her when she didn't even have the opportunity to feel the same conflict.

Still, as they made their way back to the group, Ryan stayed close by her side. The others were still laughing, engrossed in their conversation over another round of drinks, oblivious to the emotional storm that had just passed for Maya. He kept a protective eye on her, watching for any sign that she was struggling again, but she managed to slip back into the group without much notice. She was good at hiding behind a mask when she needed to.

They resumed the game, and Ryan's shoulder brushed hers every now and then, just to remind her he was there if she needed him. He knew she wasn't ready to talk about it yet—he could see the way she held herself a little tighter, trying to keep it together—but he was determined to be there when she was.

As he watched her, his thoughts drifted back to their earlier conversation, the way she had melted into his arms when she needed comfort. He had seen Maya at her most vulnerable, and it stirred something deep in him. Something he hadn't let himself fully acknowledge before.

She was beautiful tonight. Not just in the obvious way—the way her hair framed her face, the way her eyes lit up even when she was trying to hold back tears—but in the way she carried herself. Even after everything, she stood tall, determined, fierce in her own quiet way. And as much as he tried to push those feelings down, there was no denying how deeply he cared about her.

He hadn't had the chance to talk to her after his chat with Cole, which meant that he hadn't gotten to confess that he wanted to see how things went with them as a couple and his feelings for her.

Ryan's thoughts wandered as the others celebrated, their laughter echoing in the background. He couldn't stop thinking about the job offers he'd received. One from a firm in New York, one in Hartford. Both incredible opportunities, but each pulling him in opposite directions.

New York was a dream. The fast-paced energy, the endless possibilities—it was a place where his career could truly take off. But Hartford... Hartford was home. His family was there, his brother and his kids. The thought of being closer to them tugged at him in a different way. He hadn't told anyone, but his brother had offered to help him get settled if he chose Hartford, and the idea of seeing his niece and nephew grow up had been weighing on his mind.

And then there was Maya.

She was applying to firms in New York, and the truth was, he didn't want to be far from her. Not anymore. He had been hoping on her getting those job offers almost as much as she herself had been.

Ryan watched Maya as she took her turn bowling, her brow furrowed in concentration as she lined up her shot. Despite everything she was going through, she still threw herself into the moment, trying to keep up the mask of normalcy. But he could see the exhaustion creeping into her features, the weight of that rejection still hanging heavily.

She turned back toward him after knocking down a few pins, flashing him a brief smile. He gave her a thumbs-up, trying to convey without words that he was there for her.

As the night wore on, Ryan found himself gravitating toward her, staying close enough that she didn't have to carry the burden of pretending she was okay. When the others joked or laughed, he'd glance her way, watching for any sign that she might be ready to talk. But he didn't push.

At one point, Maya leaned against the table, her arms crossed, eyes distant as she watched the others bowl. Ryan stepped closer, his question low when he spoke. "You alright?"

She nodded, but it was half-hearted. "Yeah. Just... tired, I guess."

Ryan didn't press further, just nodded. He knew how it felt to carry disappointment, how heavy it could sit on your shoulders, and he wouldn't force her to unpack it until she was ready.

"I'll be right here," he murmured.

She gave him another small smile, a little more genuine this time. "I know."

As the night drew to a close, everyone started gathering their things, preparing to head out. Ryan stayed close to Maya, keeping an eye on her as she said goodbyes to the others. He knew she was still processing, still trying to figure out how to navigate the blow of the rejection.

He just hoped that her next email would be better news.

Chapter 23

Mark's POV

Mark stood under the awning of the bowling alley, watching the torrential rain pour down in sheets. The wind howled through the parking lot, and flashes of lightning illuminated the otherwise pitch-black sky. It was the kind of storm that made the whole world feel smaller, like everyone was trapped under a single, suffocating blanket of rain. He was amazed that they hadn't heard the storm from inside. Honestly, he was amazed the place was still open and had power.

"Are we ever gonna get out of here?" Emily asked, shivering a little beside him as she pulled her jacket tighter. Mark put his arm around her shoulders, pulling her closer to keep her warm. She turned into him, smiling gently.

Ryan was already tapping through his phone. "I've tried every ride-share app. Nothing's coming through. Looks like we're stuck unless we want to try driving back ourselves. I didn't bring my car tonight, though."

"Perfect," Shelby muttered, staring out at the downpour. "Carly's and Mark and Emily's apartments are the closest, but there's no way we're getting back in this mess unless we want to swim home."

Carly looked over at Shelby, raising an eyebrow. "Someone can crash on my couch. It's not a big apartment or the most comfortable couch, but it's better than braving the storm."

Shelby nodded in agreement. "Okay, yeah, that's a good idea. I'll take you up on that."

Mark glanced over at the others. "Andy and Brandon, you guys good or do you need to get somewhere?"

“Nah, we’re good. Raina lives nearby, so we’re gonna head there now before it gets worse,” Andy said, referencing his new girlfriend as he looked up from his phone and threw his jacket over his head. “She said she has a place for Brandon, too. Be safe, everyone.” Then he turned and made a dash into the rain with Brandon in tow.

Mark turned back to the remaining group—Ryan, Maya, and Emily. The rain was coming down harder now, and it didn’t look like it was letting up anytime soon. Maya, standing just a little apart from everyone, had a distant look on her face. She hadn’t said much since they left the alley, but Mark noticed the tight grip she had on her phone.

He could sense something was off. "You good, Maya?"

She blinked and looked up, trying to force a smile. "Yeah, just... thinking."

Mark nodded, but he knew there was more to it than that. He glanced at Ryan, whose gaze kept drifting toward her as well. It wasn’t hard to see the tension between them, even if they weren’t saying anything out loud. Something was brewing, not just in the storm outside, but in the air between them.

Ryan stepped forward, his eyes on Mark. “What about you guys? Any ideas how to get back?”

Mark shrugged. “Maya can come crash at ours. She can stay in the spare room and we’ll just boot you to the couch.” He turned to look at her “Maya, you’re welcome to come. If you’re okay with that. I did bring my car, but I’m not sure what the roads are gonna look like in all this.”

Maya hesitated for a moment, then nodded. "Thanks, Mark. I really appreciate that."

"No problem," Mark replied, giving her a reassuring smile. “It’s better than being stuck out here all night.”

THE RAIN LASHED AGAINST the car windows as they drove, the wipers barely able to keep up with the downpour. Mark focused on the road ahead, trying to navigate the near-zero visibility. His knuckles whitened on the steering wheel, but he stayed calm. Everyone was quiet, lost in their own thoughts. Even Emily, who normally kept up conversation, was uncharacteristically silent.

Maya sat in the back with Ryan, staring out the rain-streaked window. She was tense, her hands clasped tightly in her lap. Ryan sat beside her, his own hands resting on his knees, but every now and then, his gaze would flicker toward her, concern etched on his face.

Mark kept his eyes on the road but couldn't help noticing the undercurrent between them. He'd seen them disappear earlier in the night but hadn't said anything. They hadn't been gone long, but Maya had seemed more withdrawn afterwards.

"Almost there," he said, mostly to break the silence. His apartment was only a few blocks away, but with the storm, it felt like they were navigating through a maze of water and wind.

Finally, they pulled into the lot, parking under a small overhang to minimize the drenching they'd get running inside.

"Alright, everyone out," Mark said, grabbing the keys and stepping out into the rain. They made a mad dash for the entrance, rushing inside and shaking off the rainwater like drenched animals.

He led them all into the living room, grabbing a few towels from the hall closet and tossing them around. "Dry off. I'll get some blankets and pillows for everyone."

Ryan and Maya both nodded, gratefully accepting the towels. Emily had already claimed a spot on a kitchen stool, tugging off her soggy shoes and drying her hair in the towel.

Mark watched as Ryan tugged off his own shoes and wet socks and padded away, returning moments later and giving Maya a shirt of his to change into. He suppressed a smile at the gesture as Maya padded away toward the guest room with a quiet thanks. He could tell Ryan was distracted, his mind clearly on something else—perhaps whatever had had them sneaking off earlier.

Mark busied himself by throwing towels on the floor to soak up some of the mess while Emily wandered into their room to get some dry clothes for herself. Once that was sorted, he followed her lead and did the same.

"Now might be as good a time as any to just go talk to her." He told Ryan as he passed.

Ryan smiled wryly, "Yeah, maybe you're right."

Mark chuckled to himself as he went to get ready for bed.

Chapter 24

Maya's POV

Maya stood in the guest room, pulling Ryan's shirt over her head. It was soft and worn, the fabric carrying the faintest scent of him. She caught a glimpse of herself in the mirror, the oversized shirt hanging loosely over her frame. The hem brushed her thighs, barely covering her.

She clenched her jaw, feeling a wave of emotion washing over her. Tonight had been a rollercoaster. The disappointment of the email from Hayes & Martin still weighed heavily on her, but the way Ryan had been there for her and held her while she cried had made everything a little easier to bear.

A soft knock at the door startled her.

"Come in," she called, her heart skipping a beat when she realized who it must be.

Ryan stepped into the room, and the sight of him made her breath catch in her throat. He was wearing nothing but a pair of joggers, his chest bare, skin still slightly damp. His hair was tousled, his jaw clenched as his eyes swept over her, taking in the sight of her in his shirt.

For a moment, neither of them said anything. The air between them was thick, charged with electricity. His gaze lingered on her legs, then slowly traveled back up to meet her eyes. The lust in his expression was unmistakable, his jaw tight as though he was holding himself back.

She felt a rush of something igniting deep inside her. "I... I feel bad about taking your bed," she said softly.

Ryan shook his head, his voice low and rough. "Don't worry about it. It's no big deal. I'll be fine."

Maya hesitated for a moment, then took a deep breath and met his eyes. "You could stay," she offered quietly, her heart galloping as the words left her mouth. "We could... share it. But I understand if you want to keep your distance."

His eyes darkened, and he took a step closer, his expression conflicted. "Maya," he began in almost a growl. "It's not that. Trust me, I don't want to keep my distance from you. But I don't want to take advantage of what you're feeling right now. You've been through a lot."

Maya's heart fluttered at the raw honesty in his tone. She could see how much he was holding back, the tension rippling through his body as he stood only a few feet away from her. His hands were clenched at his sides, like he was physically restraining himself from reaching out to her.

"I don't feel like you're taking advantage of me," she whispered, not sure where her sudden confidence came from as she took a small step toward him. "Maybe I've wanted this for a long time."

Ryan let out a breath, his gaze locked on hers as though he was fighting some internal battle. "Maya, if we do this—if we cross that line, there's no going back."

"I know," she said softly, stepping even closer, feeling the magnetic pull between them. "I don't want to go back."

Her words seemed to break something in him. In an instant, Ryan's hand was on her waist, pulling her against him. His lips crashed down on hers with a force that left her breathless, and she melted into him, her arms winding around his neck as she kissed him back with everything she had. The tension that had been building between them for so long finally snapped, and she could feel the raw desire radiating from him, matching her own.

Suddenly, they were on the bed, Ryan moving over her, his body pressing her down into the mattress. Her hands were everywhere—on his chest, his shoulders, his back—trying to pull him closer, to feel more of him. He groaned against her lips as her fingers grazed the firm muscles of his back, and the sound sent a jolt straight through her.

She arched up into him, desperate to feel more, her body instinctively seeking friction as the ache of desire intensified. She could feel just how much he wanted her, his body hard and unyielding against hers, and the sensation only fueled the fire inside her. She let out a soft gasp as his hand slid under her shirt, his fingers trailing over her skin, leaving a trail of sparks in their wake.

"Maya," he whispered, sounding ragged as he broke the kiss, resting his forehead against hers. "We don't have to rush this."

She shook her head, her breath coming in quick, shallow gasps as she met his gaze. "I want this, Ryan. I want you."

That was all the encouragement he needed. His lips were back on hers, more urgent this time, and she responded with equal fervor. Every touch, every kiss, felt electric, like they were setting each other on fire. The world outside the room faded away, and all that mattered was the way his body fit against hers, the way his hands moved over her, the way he made her feel alive in a way she hadn't felt in so long.

As they moved together, lost in the moment, Maya couldn't help but feel like everything had led to this—every glance, every moment of tension, every unspoken word. There was no more hesitation, no more holding back.

There was no more room for denying that they fit together like two pieces of a puzzle. Maya had never felt such pleasure and desire in her entire life and could not get enough.

As they came together, he alternated between whispering her name like a prayer and worshiping every inch of her skin he could reach with his mouth.

She felt herself getting lost in the sensation of him, touching every inch of skin she could reach as she tried to pull him impossibly closer.

Maya awoke to the sound of a phone ringing, a persistent, jarring noise that cut through the haze of sleep. She blinked slowly, the dim morning light filtering through the curtains, casting a soft glow around the room. She was nestled comfortably in Ryan's bed, wearing nothing but his shirt, which was rumpled but still smelled faintly of him. His body behind her made her feel cocooned and safe.

As the phone continued to ring, she groggily reached over, her mind still foggy from sleep, and picked up the phone from the nightstand. Tyler's face appeared on the screen and his voice came through the speaker with a mix of concern and cheerfulness.

"Ryan! Just checking in. Heard about the storm and closures.... Oh, hey, Maya! Everything okay there?" Tyler's words went from worried to inviting. He didn't miss a beat to find Maya answering his brother's phone.

Maya's eyes widened as she slowly realized where she was. She was in Ryan's bed, wearing his shirt, and now answering his phone. Her heart skipped a beat, and she glanced back to see Ryan stirring behind her, his hand reaching out instinctively to pull her closer before he was fully awake.

"Uh, hey Tyler," Maya said, slightly flustered as she tried to gather her thoughts. She'd only met Tyler once before when he had come to California with his family briefly a few years ago, but she had still been with Cole then. "Yeah, we're okay. I didn't realize there were closures. We hadn't heard about that yet."

Ryan's hand paused midway around her torso, and he looked at her with sleep-laden eyes. His gaze fell on the phone in her hand, then back to her. He gave her a sleepy, reassuring smile and murmured, "Don't worry about it. I'll talk to him."

Without missing a beat, Ryan took the phone from Maya's hand and shifted the camera so she was no longer in it, his expression shifting to one of relaxed familiarity as he greeted his brother. He chatted with Tyler briefly, discussing the storm and the kids.

Even though Ryan seemed perfectly at ease, Maya's cheeks flushed with embarrassment as she thought about how intimate and unplanned this situation was. She tucked herself against his side, pulling up the sheets so nothing was visible on screen. Ryan wrapped the arm that wasn't holding his phone around her and held her closer, fingers rubbing her bare skin where her shirt had ridden up.

Ryan kept the call short and placed the phone back on the nightstand before turning his attention back to Maya. He brushed a strand of hair from her face, his touch tender and lingering.

"So," Ryan said warmly, "looks like we had a surprise this morning."

Maya smiled, feeling a mix of nerves and excitement. "Yeah, seems like it. I'm sorry. I didn't mean to answer your phone like that. I didn't realize."

Ryan chuckled softly, his eyes twinkling with amusement. "It's okay. You look incredible in my shirt, by the way."

Maya felt a rush of relief at his compliment, and she smiled shyly. "Thank you. It's really nice to wake up like this."

Ryan's hand reached out, gently cupping her face as he leaned in. "Just nice?" he joked. "I'm glad we're here together. And if you need to talk or just be close, I'm here. We don't have to rush anything."

Maya's heart fluttered at his words. "I really appreciate that, Ryan."

Their eyes locked, and the intensity of the moment pulled them back together. Ryan's lips brushed against hers, tenderly at first, but quickly building in urgency. As they kissed, Maya's hands roamed over his chest, feeling his skin beneath her fingertips. The touch of him, his embrace, made her forget about everything else.

Their kisses grew deeper, more passionate, as they pulled each other closer, their bodies pressed together. Everything seemed to fade away, leaving just the two of them, tangled in each other's arms. Somehow, Maya still wanted him so much it was almost painful.

They broke the kiss briefly, their foreheads resting against each other as they breathed heavily. "I guess this was one way of telling you that I really want to see where things go with us," Ryan said softly. "Though that's a conversation I should have made sure we had last night before getting... distracted."

Maya smiled at him. "Yeah, but I'm not complaining. I really want to see where this goes, too."

As their hands continued to explore each other's bodies, their kisses grew more fervent. The connection between them was undeniable, a mix of emotions and physical desire that brought them even closer. Despite the unexpected turn of events, Maya felt a deep sense of belonging and intimacy that she hadn't experienced before.

Ryan's POV

He lay still and content as the early morning light filtered through the curtains, casting a soft glow around the room. The storm had settled, leaving a peaceful calm outside. Maya was draped across him, her head resting on his chest, one leg tangled with his as she gently traced circles on his skin. He tightened his arm around her, pulling her closer as they lay in comfortable silence, basking in the feeling of each other.

Maya let out a soft sigh, her breath tickling his skin. "I'm grateful that the storm's given us an extra morning off," she murmured, glancing at her phone. "Classes are canceled. Flooding everywhere. That said, I feel horrible for admitting that while knowing that there's been damage."

Ryan felt a weight lift at the news. "An unexpected day off sounds pretty perfect right about now, but I get what you mean."

She shifted slightly, propping her chin up to look at him. There was a soft smile on her face, but beneath it, something uncertain lingered. "So... now what? Are we, um, together?" she asked quietly, her fingers brushing against his chest, as if she wasn't quite sure what the morning meant for them.

Before Ryan could respond, his phone started vibrating relentlessly on the nightstand. He groaned, reaching for it without disturbing Maya too much. He unlocked it to see messages from his family. Tyler had sent a simple text first: "*You and Maya, huh? LOL Good morning from the kids.*"

But it was followed by a string of texts from his mother and sister.

Ryan chuckled, holding up the phone for Maya to see. "Looks like Tyler couldn't resist sharing our morning with the whole family."

Her eyes widened in shock. "Oh my god, are you serious?" she asked, sitting up slightly, now fully straddling his waist. Ryan momentarily found himself distracted by her position on his lap but forced himself to focus.

"Yup," Ryan answered, scrolling through the messages. "Looks like my mom's been trying to reach me, and my sister's already in full gossip mode."

Maya groaned, dropping her head onto his shoulder with a mix of laughter and embarrassment. "Well, this is going to be fun then. What are you going to tell them?"

Ryan gently lifted her chin, looking into her eyes. "What do *you* want me to tell them? I'd love to tell them about my girlfriend, but that's up to you if you're comfortable with that."

She hesitated, picking her nails. "I don't want to hide anything, but... will they think this is weird with our past? I mean, it *is* a little weird, right?" She sounded uncertain and Ryan could see the vulnerability in her gaze.

He brushed a strand of hair behind her ear. "We don't have to figure everything out right now. But..." He paused, thinking. "I'm not going to lie to them. If they ask, I can just say that you're important to me, and we're figuring things out, if you'd prefer."

Maya gave a small, appreciative smile. "That sounds... fair. I don't want to pressure you, but I am planning on being in NYC no matter what. I got an offer from a firm that I wasn't planning on needing to take but depending on what happens with Wexler & Greene I might have to. You have so many options, though, that I don't want you to base your decision on me... or be ashamed of this."

"Ashamed?" Ryan pulled her closer, his hand tracing her back. "Maya, there's nothing about this that I regret. You mean a lot to me. And I'm not going to hide that from anyone, titles or not. I was contemplating New York long before this semester. You were right before. I did apply there for a reason. I want to be close to my family, but I'm torn because Hartford might be *too* close, you know? New York seemed like a perfect balance. Ideal for corporate risk management and close enough to visit without being right there."

She smiled softly, pressing her forehead to his. "I'm glad we're on the same page. Maybe after a few dates we can make this official?"

He kissed her temple, feeling the softness of her skin against his lips. "Done. Now, maybe we should get ready before I get distracted again."

They reluctantly pulled away from each other, dressing in comfortable silence. Ryan couldn't help but steal glances at her as she moved around the room, wearing his shirt and nothing else. There was something so intimate about seeing her like this, the easy familiarity between them. He knew they had more to talk about, more to navigate, but for now, this quiet moment was enough.

Once they were dressed, Ryan in a simple tee and joggers, and Maya still wearing his shirt but adding her pants, they headed out to the living room. The smell of coffee hit them immediately, and they found Mark and Emily already sitting at the small dining table, sipping their mugs.

Mark was the first to look up, a knowing smirk on his face, purposefully looking from the couch that clearly hadn't been slept in to them. "Morning," he said, dragging out the word in a way that made Ryan want to roll his eyes.

Emily glanced between them with raised brows, clearly trying to suppress a grin. "Good sleep?" she asked innocently.

Ryan felt Maya's hand brush against his as they walked over to the kitchen counter. He leaned in slightly, lowering his whispering his words just for her with a grin. "Well, they're definitely not going to let this slide."

She giggled quietly, nudging him with her shoulder as they grabbed mugs of coffee.

Mark continued to eye them with amusement. "You know, I'm not going to make this awkward," he started, taking another slow sip of coffee. "But since we're all friends here... Does this mean the two of you are finally going to admit you're *more* than just friends?"

Ryan, without missing a beat, met Mark's gaze and replied steadily. "Actually, yeah. We've talked about it, and we're figuring things out. No labels yet, but we're not going to hide what we are feeling either."

Maya's hand found his under the counter, giving it a reassuring squeeze. He looked down at her, seeing the gratitude in her eyes.

Mark raised his hands in mock surrender, grinning. "Hey, no judgment here. Just glad to see you happy."

Emily smirked, leaning back in her chair. "Took you two long enough. I mean, we all kind of saw this coming."

Ryan laughed, glancing at Maya. "Well, better late than never, right?"

Maya shook her head with a smile, clearly amused but also grateful for how easily things had settled. “I guess so.”

They all settled into a comfortable rhythm, talking and laughing about nothing in particular. Ryan was still aware of the unanswered messages on his phone, but right now, he didn’t mind. There would be time to deal with his family later. For now, he was content to enjoy a lazy day.

Chapter 25

Ryan's POV

The streets were still damp from the rain, but the clouds had finally parted, leaving behind a bright afternoon sun that gleamed off the wet pavement. Ryan had just dropped Maya off at her apartment. The look she gave him before she went inside stuck with him—the soft, unspoken promise that what had happened between them meant something. But there was still so much up in the air, so many decisions to make, especially with his job offers looming over his head.

As he pulled back up to Mark's apartment, his phone buzzed again, this time from Tyler. He leaned back in the driver's seat, exhaling slowly before answering the call.

"Hey, man," Ryan greeted, rubbing his hand over his face. "What's up?"

"Just checking in. Didn't hear from you after this morning," Tyler's teasing lilt came through the phone. "Heard you had an interesting wake-up call or something."

Ryan couldn't help but chuckle, even though the memory still made him shake his head. "Yeah, thanks for that, by the way. Maya answering my phone in bed wasn't exactly how I pictured breaking the news to you guys."

"Hey, don't blame me. You left your phone lying around, and we were worried with all the flooding and stuff. I just wasn't expecting to see that when I called." There was a pause, then Tyler added, more serious now, "But, all joking aside, it was good to see you two like that. You've been pining over her for long enough."

Ryan leaned his head back against the seat, staring up at the roof of his car. "Yeah... well, it's still unofficial for now. She doesn't want to influence my choices for after graduation."

"I can respect that. But you're happy, right? That's what matters."

"Yeah." Ryan's chest tightened. He thought about how it felt waking up with Maya next to him, how natural it had seemed, despite the months of dancing around their feelings. "I am. Happier than I've been in a long time."

"I'm glad," Tyler said, but there was a shift in his tone, like he could sense that something was still on Ryan's mind. "But about those after graduation choices... you know that we'd be happy to have you back home, but New York is only a few hours away and we'd be just as happy to have you just be that close, too. Whatever is best for you is all any of us really want, you know."

Ryan sighed, glancing out the window. He had been turning it over in his head all day, but he knew he couldn't put off the decision any longer. "I've made up my mind," he finally said.

Tyler didn't say anything for a moment, waiting for Ryan to continue.

"I'm going to take the position in New York," Ryan said, the words hanging in the air between them. "I've been going back and forth, trying to decide between Hartford and New York, but I think it's the right move. New York has more opportunities; more experience to be gained. I'll still be close enough to Hartford that I can visit on weekends or whenever."

"I thought that might be the case," Tyler responded, no hint of judgment in his words. "Congrats, man."

"Thank you," Ryan said, more confident now that he'd said it aloud. "It's only two or so hours away, and it feels like the right choice. The company is a bigger name with more connections. I need to start building my career, and I think New York's the best place for that."

"Does Maya know yet?" Tyler asked.

Ryan shook his head, even though Tyler couldn't see him. "Not yet. She's still waiting to hear back from Wexler & Greene. I didn't want to tell her until I knew for sure, but... I don't know, Ty. I feel like New York's going to be good for me. I don't want to wait around for what might or might not happen with that."

"Yeah, I get it. But what about Maya? You guys just started figuring things out. You think you'll be able to make it work with you in New York?"

Ryan hesitated. "I think so. We haven't really had that conversation yet. I didn't want to pressure her with all that while she's still figuring out her own next steps. I do know she got some offers she was less enthusiastic about in New York, though, so I think she'll be heading there regardless."

"Well, at least you're not going too far. You can still see her. And if she gets that job in New York she's hoping for... well, then it's perfect, right? And even if she doesn't get it now, jobs aren't permanent. She can always change companies once she is there, boots on the ground and whatnot." Tyler responded positively.

"Yeah," Ryan said, though the uncertainty in his chest didn't fully fade. "I just don't want to screw this up. We've barely even started, and now... I know she was adamant that she didn't want to influence my decision, but I don't think she has. Not that much. I think I would have made this choice regardless."

"You're not screwing anything up," Tyler assured him. "You're just taking the next step in your career. If it's meant to work, it'll work. Maya's not going to stop you from choosing what's best for you. Besides, two hours is nothing. We'll still see you a hell of a lot more than we do right now."

Ryan chuckled. "Yeah, you're right. It's just... a lot. I haven't even had time to process everything."

"Well, you've got a day off now, so take a breather," Tyler said, his voice lightening again. "And hey, next time I call, I expect a heads-up if someone else is going to answer your phone, alright?"

Ryan laughed, shaking his head. "I'll keep that in mind."

"Take care, man. And congrats on the New York gig. Proud of you."

"Thanks, Ty. Talk soon."

Ryan hung up the phone, leaning back in his seat for a moment longer. He knew he needed to tell Maya about his decision, but part of him worried how she'd take it—especially after her comment this morning. He ran a hand through his hair, staring out at the city beyond the windshield.

New York felt like the right decision for him, and he hoped that it would work out for Maya, too.

Maya's POV

Maya unlocked the front door and stepped into the apartment, her mind buzzing from the past twenty-four hours. Shelby was sitting on the couch, flipping through a magazine, but she looked up as soon as Maya entered.

"Hey! You're back. Glad to see you survived!" Shelby grinned, putting the magazine aside.

Maya dropped her purse by the door, already feeling her face get hot at the mention of Ryan. "It was... a night, that's for sure." She smirked, pulling off her jacket and sitting beside Shelby. "Long story short, we stayed at Mark's, and I ended up sharing Ryan's bed."

Shelby's eyes widened, leaning in with anticipation. "And?"

"Let's just say it was a little more than sleeping."

Shelby let out a laugh and nudged Maya playfully. "You're really just going to drop that and not give me details?"

Maya opened her mouth to respond when her phone buzzed in her hand. Glancing down, she saw the email notification from Wexler & Greene. Her breath hitched. "Oh my god."

"What?" Shelby asked, suddenly sitting up straighter.

"It's Wexler & Greene..." Maya's hands shook as she opened the email. Her eyes scanned the words, and as soon as she saw *offer*, she jumped to her feet. "I GOT IT! I GOT THE OFFER!"

Shelby let out a squeal and threw her arms around Maya. "Maya, that's amazing! You did it! That's the dream job!"

Maya couldn't stop smiling, her heart soaring. "I can't believe it. This was what I have been hoping for!" She took a deep breath, trying to process the news, rereading the email to make sure she had read it correctly. "I start right after graduation if I accept."

Shelby pulled back, grinning from ear to ear. "You have to accept, right? I mean, it's New York!"

Maya's smile wavered as her thoughts turned to Ryan. "Yeah... New York." She sat back down, a mixture of excitement and nervousness bubbling in her chest. "But... I don't know what Ryan's plans are. I told him pretty plainly that I was going to New York one way or another, but I didn't want to influence his choice."

Shelby gave her a soft look, understanding the weight of her words. "You'll figure it out. Just talk to him. I know he was gunning for New York or Hartford, so even if he ends up there that wouldn't be too far away."

"Maybe you're right," Maya admitted. "I just can't believe it. I really did it."

Her phone buzzed again, and this time, it was a text from Ryan: *Hey, want to grab dinner? I know a place that's still open after the storm.*

Maya's heart skipped a beat. "Ryan just asked if I want to get dinner."

Shelby's grin returned. "Perfect. Go out, celebrate, and you can tell him about the offer when it feels right. Just... enjoy it for now. And make sure you make your decision for you, even though I think we both know what that decision is."

Maya hugged her friend, wondering how on earth she got so lucky.

Chapter 26

Maya's POV

Maya stood by the door, fiddling with the hem of her jacket as Shelby leaned against the counter, a knowing grin on her face.

"Are you nervous or something?" Shelby teased. "You've stayed with him twice now. Dinner should be a breeze."

Maya shot her a playful glare. "It's not like that." But she knew it was. Tonight felt... different. "I just want everything to go well."

Shelby wiggled her eyebrows. "It will. But if you're nervous, maybe tell him you love the shirt he loaned you. Bet he's thinking about that."

Maya's cheeks flushed, and she opened her mouth to retort when a knock on the door saved her from Shelby's teasing.

"That's him." Maya grabbed her purse, turning to Shelby one last time. "Don't wait up."

Shelby waved her off with a smirk. "Oh, I won't. But have fun."

Maya opened the door to find Ryan standing there, casual in a dark gray jacket and jeans, but as soon as their eyes met, she noticed the subtle tension in his shoulders. She smiled at him, feeling the nerves she'd been trying to push aside resurface. "Hey."

"Hey," Ryan greeted her, a small smile playing on his lips. "Ready to go?"

She nodded, stepping out and letting him guide her to his car. As they drove, Maya tried to relax, but she couldn't help noticing the way his fingers gripped the steering wheel a little tighter than usual. He was tense—more so than she'd seen him lately—and it made her wonder if there was something on his mind. She wanted to ask, but instead, she kept her own excitement bottled up, waiting for the right moment to tell him about her offer.

"So," she started, hoping to break the silence, "Shelby couldn't resist teasing me before I left."

Ryan glanced at her, his expression softening. "Oh yeah? What about?"

"You know, just... us," Maya said with a light laugh, though her heart was racing. "She thinks I'm nervous, but I think it's just the job stuff still lingering in my head."

Ryan's mouth twitched, almost like he wanted to laugh but was holding it back. "Yeah, that makes sense. Lots to figure out."

Maya shifted in her seat, deciding to change the subject. "Right... so how's everything with your sister? The wedding is coming up soon, isn't it?"

"Yeah," Ryan said, a little more relaxed now. "It's in about four weeks. She's been texting nonstop about last-minute things—flowers, seating arrangements, that sort of thing. My mom's losing her mind over it, but it should be fun. I'm happy for her."

Maya smiled, the thought of a family wedding adding to the quiet joy she felt. "I bet it'll be beautiful. Are you in the wedding party?"

"Groomsman," he said with a chuckle. "Mostly means I'm in charge of keeping my brother from causing too much chaos. But my soon-to-be brother-in-law is a good guy and we all like him, so I hope it all goes well."

"Tyler?" Maya grinned, remembering the call that morning. "I'm sure he'll be on his best behavior."

Ryan shook his head, smiling now. "You don't know my brother. Best behavior isn't really in his vocabulary."

They continued driving, the conversation helping to ease some of the tension between them. Maya found herself feeling a little lighter, but the thought of the email from Wexler & Greene still lingered in the back of her mind. She wanted to tell him—needed to—but she also didn't want to rush it.

The restaurant they were heading to was farther out, a small place that had managed to stay open despite the storm. When they finally arrived, the lights from the parking lot cast a warm glow over the building, and Maya could feel her heart thudding as they walked in together.

A friendly hostess greeted them and led them to a cozy booth by the window. As soon as they sat down, Maya noticed the familiar tension creeping back into Ryan's posture. He glanced out the window, his jaw tightening slightly as if he was lost in thought.

"Do you want a drink to start?" the hostess asked, handing them their menus.

"Uh, yeah," Ryan said, shaking off whatever had been on his mind. "I'll have a beer."

Maya glanced at him, trying to gauge his mood. "I'll just have a glass of wine," she added with a small smile.

Once the hostess left, the silence between them felt heavier than before. Maya swallowed, knowing it was now or never to bring up the offer.

"Maya, I—" he suddenly started.

"Ryan," she started at the same time.

They both stopped, before chuckling.

"Please, ladies first." Ryan gestured at her to continue.

"I got an email today." She stated, meeting his eyes. "From Wexler & Greene."

His brow furrowed slightly, the tension in his body shifting as he leaned in just a little closer. "Yeah? What did they say?"

Maya took a deep breath. "I got the offer."

A smile spread across his face, and he grabbed a hold of her hand on the table. "That's amazing, Maya. Congratulations."

She smiled. "Thank you. It's... everything I wanted."

Ryan nodded, but she noticed the way his hand flexed in hers. There was something else on his mind.

"I haven't accepted yet, though," she admitted. "I mean, I'm going to, but... I wanted to talk to you first. About your plans."

Ryan's eyes softened, and for the first time that night, some of the tension seemed to leave him. "I've been thinking a lot about that." He leaned back, running a hand through his hair. "I've been torn between Hartford and New York for a while, but after talking to my brother earlier... I'm going to take the New York offer."

Maya's heart skipped a beat. "New York?"

"Yeah." He gave her a small smile. "It's what I want. The experience there is going to be unmatched, and it just... feels right."

Relief flooded through her, but it was mixed with a surge of emotion she wasn't entirely prepared for. "So... we'll both be in New York City."

Ryan's eyes met hers, and for a moment, they just stared at each other, the weight of what that meant hanging between them.

"Yeah," he said softly. "We will."

Their drinks arrived then, interrupting the moment, but the air between them felt different now—heavier, more certain.

Maya took a sip of her wine, her mind still racing as she processed everything. They were both going to New York. It was real. All the uncertainty that had been weighing on her shoulders seemed to lift, replaced with a quiet but growing sense of excitement.

“It's actually part of the reason I wanted to take you on a proper date tonight.” Ryan continued. “You mentioned earlier that you didn't want to influence me, but I think I would have gone this route regardless. You also said that we might need to have a few dates before making things official.”

His eyes bored into hers with an intensity that left her breathless.

“I wanted to bring you on a date to tell you that this may be me being brash or reckless or moving way too fast, but I would love for you to be my girlfriend. I would love for us to go to New York together. As a couple.”

Maya's heart practically stopped at the same time her head bobbed up and down. "Yes." She said, squeezing his hand that was still in hers. "I would love that more than anything. Let's do it."

His responding smile made her heart melt in absolute bliss.

"Here's to New York," she said, raising her glass with a small, nervous smile.

Ryan raised his beer and clinked it gently against her glass. "To New York."

Their dinner was wonderful, and Maya felt more relaxed and happier than she had in months as they ate and chatted and planned. The fact that they were making plans, albeit theoretical, for life together in New York City felt wild to her. She felt like they were moving fast to be talking about living together but simultaneously felt that they had known each other and had been building to this for so long.

Maya felt the buzz of the restaurant fading as they stepped into the cool night air, the conversation still buzzing in her mind as they walked toward Ryan's car, his arm wrapped firmly around her shoulders. The drive back was quieter than the drive there, but not uncomfortable—just different. A quiet kind of tension hummed between them, something unspoken but felt in the charged glances they exchanged.

Maya couldn't help but be grateful for Shelby's talk earlier, telling her that waiting around before becoming 'official' was ridiculous with how close she and Ryan already were. That advice really made Maya think about why she had wanted that, and realized it was a bit silly considering their history already.

They pulled up outside her apartment, the warm glow from the windows spilling onto the sidewalk. Shelby would be there, probably ready with some teasing remark, but Maya didn't want to think about that now. She wanted to stay in this moment with Ryan.

As they walked up to the door, the night felt heavy with possibilities. Before she could open it, Ryan's hand on her back stopped her. She turned to him, and the look in his eyes sent a shiver down her spine. His hand was warm, steady, and she felt the gentle pressure of it through her sweater.

"Maya, before we go in... I just want to say something," he started before taking a steadying breath.

Her heart leapt, caught between anticipation and fear. She nodded, searching his face for clues.

"Whatever happens next, whatever the future looks like in New York... I don't want to lose this," he said, his thumb brushing lightly against her side. "I've been thinking about it a lot. About us. And I—" He faltered for a moment, his breath hitching before he continued. "I don't want us to become pulled apart by conflicting schedules or family pressure. I don't ever want you to feel like you can't tell me what's on your mind or tell me when I've done something you don't agree with. I am not Cole. I don't want to become that person who becomes blind to the things that you want and need, okay?"

Maya's breath caught. "Okay," she whispered. "But Ryan... you just said it. You aren't Cole. You have never made me feel like what I want is unimportant or unreasonable. That being said, I promise to let you know if that starts to change. We will forge our own path forward together."

Ryan took a step closer, closing the distance between them. His hands moved to her waist, pulling her gently toward him. "Together," he said, his voice suddenly more confident. "For as long as you'll have me."

She felt a rush of relief and excitement, but also the weight of his words. This was it—this was real. Maya leaned up, closing the gap between them, her lips brushing against his in a kiss that started softly but deepened as her arms wrapped around his neck. Every touch, every movement felt charged, as if they were pouring everything they hadn't said into that kiss.

When they finally pulled apart, breathless, Ryan looked down at her, his eyes intense. "Let's go inside," he said softly.

They stepped into the apartment, Shelby nowhere to be seen for once. Maybe she had actually given them space. Maya smiled at the thought, her heart still racing from the kiss. She turned toward Ryan as he shut the door behind them, the dim light of the hallway casting soft shadows over his features.

Maya hesitated for a moment, and then, as if reading her mind, Ryan stepped forward again, his hands cupping her face. "I meant it," he whispered. "I'm all in."

Her chest swelled with emotion, and she could only nod, feeling the tears prick at her eyes. She reached up to kiss him again, softer this time but just as urgent. He pulled her closer, his hands trailing down her back as they stumbled toward the bedroom, their laughter breaking the intensity for just a moment.

Later, as they lay tangled together in the sheets, Maya rested her head on Ryan's chest, listening to the steady rhythm of his breathing. The calm after the intensity of their connection felt grounding.

She knew that they were moving way too fast. In less than 36 hours they had gone from friends to lovers to something more. They were going to New York together. Suddenly, she didn't want to hold anything back anymore.

Maya reached up, her hand cupping his face. "I love you, Ryan," she whispered, thick with emotion.

For a moment, there was only the sound of their breathing as the words hung between them. And then, Ryan's arms wrapped tightly around her, pulling her into him as he whispered against her skin, "I love you too, Maya. More than I think I ever realized."

They held each other for a long time, the world outside fading into the background. All that mattered was this moment, this new beginning.

Epilogue

Ryan's POV

Ryan stood in the quiet of their apartment, staring at the gallery of photos on the wall. His eyes lingered on the picture from his sister's wedding—a candid shot of him and Maya laughing together, their hands intertwined. She had been stunning that day, her blue dress hugging her in all the right places, her eyes sparkling as she twirled around the dance floor.

He remembered the way his chest had tightened watching her move through the crowd, effortlessly charming his family. It was in that moment he knew, without a doubt, that she was the person he wanted to spend the rest of his life with, despite the short time they had been together at that point.

But that wasn't the only memory on display.

Next to it was a photo of them hiking in the Catskills. Maya's face was flushed from exertion, but she was grinning, standing triumphantly at the summit. He remembered that trip vividly—it had been their first real adventure after moving to New York.

They'd been overwhelmed by the hustle and bustle of the city, and he suggested a weekend getaway. They spent the days hiking and the nights huddled together by the fire, talking about everything and nothing.

His gaze drifted further down the wall. There was another picture from their trip to Boston—Maya standing outside Fenway Park, wearing his baseball cap backward, holding up a foam finger, and laughing. He could almost hear her teasing him about how "serious" he'd gotten about the game that night, and how she didn't understand why he cared so much about which team won. They had ended up getting drenched in a downpour, running through the streets like kids. It had been one of those simple, perfect moments that felt like it should have been in a movie.

Ryan smiled softly, letting the memories settle around him. Their first year in New York had been chaotic but beautiful. They'd both dived headfirst into their careers—and somehow still made time for each other. Life was good.

And their friends had found their places too. Carly, after breaking up with Rachel, had decided to move to New York herself. Her freelance work allowed her to live anywhere, and though it had been hard at first to see her and Rachel part ways, Carly had embraced the change. Ryan knew she was excited about the new start.

She was already planning to visit apartments with Shelby that weekend, and it made him happy to know that his little circle of people was slowly gathering closer together. Shelby, of course, was still completing her residency and crushing it, like always.

He smiled, thinking of their friends. Emily had married Mark—something that had surprised no one—and they were talking about starting a family. Andy and Brandon were still as inseparable as ever, surprising everyone in the best way possible with news of them becoming a couple themselves. And then there was Cole. They hadn't talked much after everything that happened, but last he heard, Cole had stayed out west, finding new opportunities with his family nearby. There was peace between them, though, a quiet understanding that life had moved forward.

He glanced further along the wall to the shot of them all at their graduation and thought that it was crazy what all had happened since that day.

The sound of the front door opening pulled him from his thoughts, and there was Maya, stepping into the apartment with her easy smile. She looked around, shrugging out of her jacket.

"Hey," she greeted, her eyes crinkling as she took him in. "What's got you so deep in thought?"

Ryan crossed the room to her, pulling her into his arms. "Just thinking about how lucky I am," he said softly.

Maya leaned into him, her arms wrapping around his waist. "What did I do to deserve that look?"

He chuckled, brushing a kiss against her temple. "Just being you."

She raised an eyebrow, her playful smile lighting up her face. "You're being mysterious today," she teased, but there was a humor in her voice that melted the edges of his nervousness. She had no idea what was coming.

Ryan pulled back slightly, letting her go as she moved to hang her jacket by the door. As she turned away, he slipped his hand into his pocket, feeling the weight of the velvet box. His heartbeat quickened. He'd been thinking about this moment for weeks—when and how to ask her the question that had been running through his mind for months now. He wanted it to be perfect, to reflect everything they had become, everything they would be together.

He glanced back at the photo wall, his eyes landing once again on the picture from his sister's wedding. He remembered watching her laugh with his family, already feeling like she was part of them, even just weeks after making things official. His niece and nephew had been immediately infatuated with her, and he had reveled in seeing her flawlessly become ingrained in the Taylors.

"Ryan?"

He turned to see her watching him curiously, her brow furrowed slightly as he mentally snapped back to the present.

He smiled, closing the distance between them. "There's something I've been meaning to ask you," he said, his voice soft but steady.

Maya's eyes widened slightly as she tilted her head, a small laugh escaping her. "You're not going to get all serious on me, are you?" she joked, but there was a flicker of something else in her gaze—anticipation, maybe. Hope.

Ryan took her hands, holding them gently as he lowered himself to one knee. The shift in her expression was instantaneous—her teasing smile faded, replaced by a wide-eyed look of disbelief.

"Maya," he began, thick with emotion, "I love you more than I could ever put into words. From the moment we reconnected—hell, even before that—you've been the person I wanted by my side. You've made me happier than I ever thought possible, and I want to spend the rest of my life with you. You make me a better man every day, and I couldn't imaging waking up without you next to me."

He pulled the velvet box from his pocket, opening it to reveal the simple but elegant ring he'd chosen weeks ago. "Will you marry me?"

Her hand flew to her mouth, tears welling up in her eyes. For a moment, she was silent, her breath catching in her throat. And then, with a small, breathless laugh, she nodded.

"Yes," she whispered, her hands trembling. "Yes, Ryan. I'll marry you."

His chest tightened with relief and joy as he slid the ring onto her finger. Rising to his feet, he pulled her into his arms, holding her tightly as she laughed through her tears.

As they stood there, wrapped in each other's arms, Ryan felt the weight of the moment sink in. This was it. This was the future he'd been waiting for, the life they'd both been working toward. Everything had fallen into place, and he couldn't wait to see what the rest of their lives would bring.

Acknowledgements

Writing *The Feelings We Can't Hide* wouldn't have been possible without the support, encouragement, and occasional reality checks from my husband and friends.

Thank you to everyone who provided any commentary on this book, as their thoughtful feedback helped shape this story into what it is today.

And to you — the reader — thank you for picking up this book. I hope it meant something to you.

Author's Note

When I started writing *The Feelings We Can't Hide*, I wanted to explore what it means to find your voice again — after heartbreak, after disappointment, after losing sight of yourself.

So often, we second guess ourselves, our choices, and our path forward. I hope that this book reminds you that the only thing we can control is ourselves and what we do next, and that's okay.

Maya's journey is personal to me in many ways, and if you saw yourself in her story, I hope it reminded you that your path matters. Always.

Thank you for being part of her story.

About the Author

Veronika Dean writes emotionally resonant stories about love, identity, and finding your way back to yourself. When not writing, she can usually be found with a coffee in hand, chasing after her kiddos or dogs, or working on the next book.

Connect on Instagram @veronika.dean.author or Tiktok @veronika.dean.author and stay tuned for new upcoming projects!

Loved the book? Let others know!

Reviews help other readers discover *The Feelings We Can't Hide* — if you enjoyed the story, please consider leaving a short review on Amazon or Goodreads.

Even just a sentence or star rating means the world to an indie author.

I appreciate you all so much. Until next time.

www.ingramcontent.com/pod-product-compliance
Lightning Source LLC
LaVergne TN
LVHW010652110826
845149LV00014B/3059

* 9 7 8 1 9 7 2 9 3 8 0 0 3 *